Colin R. Parsons is an author of action-packed, and exciting books for children and young adults. He writes in many genres: sci-fi, fantasy, steampunk and the supernatural – and has a steady stream of fans. He loves writing, but also enjoys reading too.

Colin was born and still lives in South Wales with his wife Janice. If you want to find out more, check out his website.

www.colinrparsons.com

By the same author

House of Darke

To Isaac
Best Wishes

D.I.S.C
Direct Interface Shadow
Control

Colin R. Parsons

D.I.S.C
Direct Interface Shadow Control

Pegasus

A CIP catalogue record for this title is
available from the British Library

ISBN: 978 1 91090 304 9

Pegasus is an imprint of
Pegasus Elliot MacKenzie Publishers Ltd.
www.pegasuspublishers.com

First Published in 2017

Pegasus
Sheraton House Castle Park
Cambridge CB3 0AX England

Printed & Bound in Great Britain

Dedication

For Amaya May Parsons – a new reading journey
awaits!

Acknowledgements

I would like to thank the following people for allowing me to use their names: Keiron Evans – thank you for being such a good friend, and thanks for the huge support you've always given. Also, Stephen Green, for allowing me to use part of your name for a character in this adventure.

Chapter 1

Buried in the mud

The bell was just about to go as Joseph gingerly finished up his work. Joseph Lanes was in his history class, and the fear had been building inside for the past half an hour. He dreaded the last bell every day. To everyone else it was a fantastic release to a long boring school day – but not to him. This signal only meant one thing and his heart skipped a beat just thinking about it.

BRRRRRIIINNGGG! There it was and his stomach was writhing in knots. He tried to contain the look of worry on his distraught face.

'All right, class, put away your books and walk out in single file please. Don't forget your homework,' Mr Brown, the history teacher, reminded them. This was met with an overwhelming sigh. 'No running… Hemmings, the bus will still be there in the next five minutes.' Alan Hemmings didn't reply, probably because he didn't want to get a detention. He didn't turn around either, and just grinned. He slowed his pace, until he was outside the classroom.

Joseph was putting away the last of his books, and zipping up his bag. He'd resigned himself to what was coming and almost blotted everything else out.

'Joseph Lanes, could you hold back a second?' Joseph was already making his way to the door. He was so immersed in his thoughts that he didn't hear the teacher. There were only two pupils left, and they were already disappearing into the hallway. 'Joseph Lanes, could you please wait a minute?' Mr Brown repeated, his voice slightly raised this time.

Joseph came back to his senses, and could feel his face tense. His stomach was doing acrobatics. What does *he* want? Haven't I got enough to deal with? The thoughts gushed through his mind. He turned around and walked up to the teacher's desk – and stood rigid. Mr Brown was still sitting, and made sure everyone else had vacated the room before he engaged the pupil. He'd kept an eye on the door making sure it was still open. It just wouldn't do to be in a room with a pupil with the door closed.

He then stood up. Joseph's history teacher was a tall lean man. He held his trademark thick, well-groomed, brown moustache. There were tinges of ginger at the ends of the bristles, which always made Joseph smile for some reason. Mr Brown's face was long too, like his body. He also had a good head of hair with a centre parting; which made his locks droop like curtains over his brows. He walked around his desk towards him. Joseph stepped back, but said nothing. The history teacher half sat on the corner of his desk – trying not to be too intimidating, and allowing a sensible space between them. Joseph waited for him to speak, terrified as to why he had to stay behind.

'Joseph, don't look so worried, lad, you haven't done anything wrong, honestly,' Mr Brown assured him – his tone was soft and friendly. He smiled which cut a curve in his cheeks. 'Sit on the table if you want.' Joseph was surprised. Mr Brown never let anyone sit on the tables in his class. So Joseph relaxed a little too and breathed easier. 'It's just…' Mr Brown paused. Joseph could see he was trying to explain something in his head first before blurting it out. 'I hear things and sometimes I see things.' He could see by the look on Joseph's face that he wasn't making any sense to him. He cleared his throat and blinked. He sucked in air and breathed out again, licking the underside of his moustache – which he always did absentmindedly, when explaining stuff in lessons.

'Joseph, what I'm trying to say is…' He felt awkward and lifted his finger to scratch the mid-section on his cheek, by the side of his nose. Again he waited and then simply came out with it. 'If anyone is hurting you, verbally or physically… or both! You know you can...' He stopped again, clearing his throat for the umpteenth time. 'Are you being bullied? At school or otherwise?' He said it and heaved his chest in relief.

'Err, huh, um… I-I'm fine, sir,' Joseph stuttered in a lie, feeling awkward. Mr Brown looked sceptical and shook his head doubtfully. He scrunched his forehead, revealing criss-cross lines.

'Are you sure, lad? Please don't hesitate to tell me if you are. I can do something about it,' he said, as convincingly as he could. But he knew, and Joseph knew, heart of hearts, that getting a pupil to admit to being bullied and stopping it completely, were two entirely different things. Joseph thought about it for just a moment and almost relented. He liked Mr Brown, who'd only ever been helpful to him. But he couldn't help him out of this particular situation. There was no way out it seemed.

'Honestly, sir, I'm fine,' he lied again and gave a reassuring forced smile.

'Well, okay, if you're sure, Joseph?' Mr Brown sighed. Joseph stood up and didn't move any further. 'All right, Joseph, you can go.'

Joseph walked out of the classroom and Mr Brown looked on helplessly – torment written all over the teacher's face. He shook his head again, and loosened his tie before stuffing papers into his briefcase. He remembered when he was the same age as Joseph, and the torment he went through.

Joseph though, was far from fine. In fact, Joseph was never safe. The end of a school day held the unavoidable fear of another beating. Not just one person, which would have been bad enough. There were always two – the McKenzie brothers. These boys were identical twins, in every evil way possible. These nasty bullies were overweight and overpowering. Their grim faces combined with a broccoli-like Afro of bushy hair. They enforced their heavy-set frames and brutal disposition to wreak havoc throughout the school. They were also never apart. No one had ever seen these two without the support of the other.

Everyone in school had dealings with them at some point. They tormented for a while and then moved onto their next victim. But Joseph, they took an extra liking to. He was their regular sports practice, and today would be no exception.

Joseph quickly walked through the gates, and where the other pupils carried on to the bus parking area, he didn't. He only lived across the way, and could easily get to his home in ten minutes. But to do this he had to cross a rough patch of ground, and that's where they always waited for him.

There was another way, but that took another half an hour, and it didn't really make any difference, because they would catch him on the other end of the estate once they found out he'd skipped his normal way home.

No, it was easier to go across the waste ground, and less humiliating. And quickly get it all over with. He walked tentatively along the path and to the open spot. He knew they were there even though he couldn't see them. They did the same thing every day, hid and expected Joseph to look relieved. Then pounce! He walked forward and they stepped out from behind an old shed.

'Hello, Joseph,' they spoke in unison. Joseph sighed as one of them, Jedd, grabbed him. By now he could tell them apart. Jedd had a small scar on his right knuckle, and that was really the only way. Jedd stepped behind him and linked his arms through, clamping him in an armlock.

'Aren't you going to fight back? This is getting boring,' Gary, the other twin, sneered. He let go with a few rabbit punches to Joseph's stomach. The pain was instant, as the bruises hadn't healed from their previous encounters. Joseph winced and bit his lip, but said nothing. Even though he'd tensed, the air was squeezed out of his lungs. He felt his knees buckle and give way.

'Are you going to cry, little man?' Gary grinned with relish, his eyes bright.

'Come on, Gary, we have to go,' Jedd rasped from behind, his rank breath filling Joseph's nostrils. Gary looked disappointed and gritted his teeth angrily, and then nodded. Jedd tossed the poor boy to the ground. But just before he left, gave him a kick in the groin for good measure. Joseph wasn't

17

expecting that, and the deep sick feeling almost made him vomit. There were giggles from the both of the bullies before they broke away and disappeared through the treeline.

Five minutes later Joseph Lanes still lay on his side, curled up in the foetal position. He eventually caught his breath. The pain was subsiding and the tears had dried around his eyes. The McKenzie brothers used less force this time, and he felt slightly relieved, and strangely happy. He wondered why they hadn't continued to pummel him, but obviously glad they didn't. They must have had somewhere to go, probably an appointment for a new brain, he thought, and a wry smile lit up his normally concrete frown. They'd thrown him in the mud but, luckily for Joseph, because it was summer, the soil was mostly dry. He rolled over onto his back and closed his eyes; the pain caught him as he twisted, making him wince. He rested his head on a small lump of grass, using it as an eco pillow – it felt good.

Now the bullies had gone, Joseph was left to ponder. He could smell a whiff of smoke in the air. There had been a spate of grass fires on the mountain in the surrounding area. It was on the news, deliberately started, by arsonists. Joseph wondered if the McKenzie brothers had anything to do with it, because recently he'd noticed a smell of smoke on their clothes too.

He dismissed it, and didn't want to think about them any more today. Today was a good day, only a small beating and no one to jeer. In the beginning there was always a crowd of pupils looking on. But after a while, and because this was becoming a regular occurrence, they got bored and didn't want to get involved anymore. He'd also deliberated about telling Mr Brown about his abusers, and nearly did in class earlier, but thought better of it. He knew his life would be more worthless than it is now. He often thought too, why they kept picking on him.

Joseph was small for his fifteen years – five foot four, and thin too – weedy. Oh, and he was ginger; all the ingredients for bully target practice, he supposed. He enjoyed computers, which made him a geek, double bully practice. He couldn't win.

He winced again; feeling sore all over from the many other encounters with the notorious two. He'd long given up on struggling to fight back. It was futile and would only give them even more reason to keep on assaulting him. In his mind he hoped and prayed they would get fed up soon, and go pick on some other weak victim. But it didn't look good and he would feel sorry for them then.

Besides the smoke, there was a smell of damp soil in his nostrils, but he was used to that, especially as he'd been beaten up in the same place, forever it seemed! His clothes felt uncomfortable as the mud began to dry. He sighed and looked at the sky. The blue of summer was being slowly stained with the clouds of billowing smoke from the distant mountain fire. Joseph could hear the faint sounds of fire engines in the background somewhere. This was getting all too familiar since the dry spell. He then realised it was time to go home, his parents would be worried. Then another feeling of dread – his mum would ask questions again.

Joseph took one more glance around. He tended to look at the surrounding trees from a different angle to everyone else. He realised he was always on the ground looking up – while everyone else was standing up looking down on him. This made him grin too, a strange thing to laugh about, but there was nothing else comical in his life.

He rubbed his ribs and looked at his shirt and trousers, shaking his head. There were dark stains on each. He closed his eyes and puffed out another long-winded breath. Besides the bullying, he would also get another telling off from his mum because his clothes, yet again, were damp and dirty. The McKenzie's were clever and always careful not to leave any marks on his face or arms. They can't be that stupid then, he thought, a grimace of anger consuming him. He knew he had to go. It was getting late, it was only the thought of moving that hindered him.

'Oh come on, Jo, get up,' he urged. He found he just didn't have the energy. He believed this is how a boxer must feel after twelve rounds in a title fight. But at least they got time to recover – he had a one-way boxing match every day. Wouldn't it be nice just to walk home normally? That stayed with him for a second and then disappeared.

The warmth of the sun on his face and stomach felt fantastic. It was as if it was recharging his batteries and healing his injuries at the same time. It would soon be the summer holidays – he perked up at the realisation. He could try to avoid the McKenzie brothers for six weeks at least. Oh, and they would also go on holidays too – giving him two weeks to enjoy the freedom of his estate.

Eventually he pushed himself up onto his elbows and looked around. Birds were chirping away in the background, and there was shuffling in the undergrowth. As he rolled his head from side to side relieving the stiffness – something glinted! Firstly he thought it might be a broken piece of glass, and nearly dismissed it altogether. But, it wasn't really sparkling he noticed… it was more like pulsing in sequence! He rubbed his eyes in case he was seeing things. No, it was still there only a matter of centimetres away.

Joseph was intrigued now, and it had his complete attention. What was it? The object was partially obscured by a muddy coating. He reached out and as he got closer… hesitated! He was sure there was warmth coming from it.

'That's strange,' he said. That's why the mud had dried and caked, even though it was in the shade. The winking object continued to mentally call him; Pick me up-Pick me up-Pick me up. Joseph's hand hovered over it, and the light pushed through the gaps in his fingers. He swallowed hard, it was a warm day, and he was thirsty, but that's not what was making his mouth dry. He could feel his heart thumping inside, as if it were trying to escape. His nerves got the better of him and his hand was shaking. He snatched it back! What was he afraid of? He'd been beaten up for God's sake – a flashing toy shouldn't scare him. But he felt it was more than that.

Joseph looked around – his bright blue eyes probed the area just in case someone was watching. What was there to be scared about? It was probably nothing, a flashlight that someone had lost for instance. The green indicator kept on pulling at him, goading him. He could just leave it there for someone else to find. It could be their problem not his, he'd got enough problems of his own.

He turned away from it and got to his feet. He took a few steps towards home and stopped! Was it worth anything? Whose was it? Joseph hovered for a few moments. Who was he kidding, he couldn't leave it – it was like a magnet? He turned and saw it still flashing away. He moved forward and dropped to his knees, it was the most excited and alive he'd felt in a long time. Joseph could feel his eyes widen and his mouth gape.

He took a deep breath and held out both hands. He bent over and leaned in closer, whilst gently raking the brown soil from around it. The damp mud clogged under his fingernails as he dug deeper. Once the thing was fully exposed, he could see its real shape. The object was a small disc of sorts, about the circumference of a coffee mug. Joseph cleared away the rest of the sticky dirt, leaving the strange object on a kind of muddy pedestal. It was slim, just a little thicker than a coffee coaster. The thing looked metal, but it was hard to see, especially as it was still covered in a thin coating of mud and dust. Joseph smiled. No one was taking this away from him. And he felt safe for some reason, he didn't know why. This disc was sending positive vibes and he was quite happy to receive them.

He looked more closely and could make out that the pulsing green light appeared to be inside a plastic lens. Must be a toy, he pondered. Not like one he'd ever seen before, though. The rest of it was made of metal, or hard plastic – to look like metal, he wasn't sure. He had to touch it.

He gingerly picked it up and weighed it, by gently suspending it up and down in his hand. He was surprised to find that it was light to hold but quite heavy looking.

He needed to wash it and see it in its full glory. Nearby there was a stream with a bridge running over it. On the other side of the bridge and only a few minutes away, was where he lived. He quickly got to the stream and shuffled down the makeshift path next to the bridge. This is where kids paddled through the summer, and he was lucky there wasn't anyone here yet. He wiped the disc with his wet hand and tried not to get it too moist – in case it messed up the electrics. He removed the excess dirt and looked underneath, but couldn't find where the batteries went. That's strange he thought. How's it powered? Maybe it's solar powered like my calculator.

Joseph held the object in his left hand and admired it for a minute. There were no real markings on it, or a serial number, or the manufacturer's logo. It was just a metallic blue coloured disc – smooth, and in the centre, the light. He didn't know what it was, but it was his now. It glinted in the sun as he rotated his hand. But the green light kept on winking at him. He loved the puzzle of finding something and not knowing what it did. The light was mesmerising, slightly raised from the rest of the disk. He felt a compulsion to touch it. Should he or shouldn't he – what harm could it do? He couldn't hold back any longer and pressed his finger over the tip... only to feel the dome. His stomach flipped!

'Huh, what just happened?' There was a definite pulse that radiated through him. He looked ahead at the bridge. Where was it? Where was the stream for that matter? In fact where was everything? He looked around and found he was in a completely different place!

Chapter 2

Ether World

Joseph couldn't quite make out what had happened, he was in a state of shock. But, what he did know, he definitely wasn't standing by the bridge near his home anymore. Where exactly was he? He was still kneeling on the ground in the same position. He looked around, but nothing appeared familiar. The white desolate and rocky terrain seemed to suck all the air out of his lungs. The vast landscape went on for miles and miles. Joseph shook his head doubtfully. He craned back his head and peered skyward – it was a vast ocean of blue with barely the contrast of a cloud. It was beautiful here, but there was no greenery, only chalky rock.

He felt the grip of panic in the pit of his stomach again, but he wasn't worried about bullies this time. This time it was fear of the unknown. He didn't know what was worse at this point. Would he rather be back there at the hands of the bullies? At least he would be near his home – not in this desolate place.

'Oh my God.' He couldn't stop the words tumbling from his mouth. 'What am I wearing?' He lifted his arms and looked at his chest and then, further down to his legs. His eyes widened and he rolled his tongue inside his cheeks. His school uniform had been totally replaced. Gone was the stained white shirt and muddied grey trousers. In its place was a kind of WHITE ARMOUR! A full body protective suit!

What? He didn't understand. It was as if he'd undressed and dressed again in the matter of a split-second. How is that possible? A smile lifted his spirits and he couldn't help feeling pleased with himself, and his new apparel. This whole situation was really bizarre. He looked further, at his feet. He was sporting white military style army boots. The first thing that popped into his mind was the Action Men figures he used to play with when he was eight. Now kept at the back of his cupboard at home. He remembered one wore a white uniform to blend in with a snowy terrain. This wasn't the arctic, though – it was definitely the desert somewhere.

'*I'm a soldier*?' Joseph felt the skin on his face crease up. Even saying the words didn't make much sense. 'If I *am* a soldier, I must be in some sort of role-play?'

One of his Xbox games did have this type of background. He realised how ridiculous he sounded, how could he be in a game? He was so confused; he instinctively lifted his finger to scratch his neck. He always did this as a habit when things were out of his control. But he couldn't, the smooth armour ran to the base of his skull, obscuring his skin. Plus the fact that he was also wearing gloves! He pulled his hand away, paused and closed his eyes for a few seconds – hoping, wishing things would go back to normal. 'This is all in my head, this is all in my head,' he repeated.

He opened his eyes again, slowly. No… it was no use, he was still here. For a moment he felt so alone and empty and thought about crying. Then he cleared his throat holding onto his last ounce of dignity.

'Bloody hell! Come on, Joseph, man up – keep it together. There's got to be a perfectly reasonable explanation for this.' He shook his head to clear his thoughts and took another look at his armour. This was one cool uniform.

'Wow.' He stared at his left hand with astonishment; the disc was still sitting there. He hadn't even noticed with everything else going on. But it wasn't pulsing anymore; it looked dead. 'It's like the thing had done its job, to get me here,' Joseph supposed. He needed to see if these things that were happening, were actually real. So he rolled his shoulders, getting the feel of his new military clothing. It felt real all right.

He'd been kneeling for so long now his thighs were burning and his leg muscles strained. He gradually pushed himself to a standing position and stretched out his chest. That felt good. 'I certainly feel real enough.' Curiously the armour was light and comfortable, like wearing a onesie – not that he ever worn one. He immediately dismissed that thought. He didn't need the McKenzie brothers to know that. They had enough reasons to beat him up already. He took a quick look around, they must be a million miles away from here, he hoped. He relaxed, and looked at his immediate surroundings. There were boulders and small rocks piled everywhere. He walked over and picked one up. It was about the size of a tennis ball. He weighed it in his hand and threw it. The small stone collided with a boulder and ricocheted. It made an echoed crack before it bounced off another and was lost.

'This all sounds and looks real enough.' Joseph reached up and touched his forehead, because he felt the pressure of something. He found a pair of goggles resting there, as if he'd always worn them. The goggles had a mouthpiece attached to it. The kind of mask mountain bikers used to filter out dust particles. This experience was getting weirder and weirder.

'What is this place?' he mumbled in a low growl. Joseph took another look at his uniform. The armour appeared to have a circular indent over his left breastplate. He squinted curiously at the empty space, and back to the disk. Then he suddenly realised that the circular indent looked approximately the same size as the object. He felt an overwhelming urge to place it there.

'What does this mean?' He plucked the disc from his left hand, with his right, and moved it towards the circular space. It began to pull away from his grip. Feeling frightened, Joseph eased it away. He thought for a moment, could it harm me? Then answered by thinking that if anything was going to harm him, it would have happened already.

'Oh what the hell,' he said, and moved it back to his chest. It automatically flipped perfectly into position as if magnetised.

At that very moment there was a shudder as if a shift in the universe! He experienced an enormous surge of energy! Something unusual and intense took place inside his body – an assertive and warm sensation. It happened so fast, it squeezed the breath out of his lungs, and made him dizzy. Joseph rested his hand on the nearest rock to steady himself. He managed to catch his breath and swallow. He blinked his eyes and opened him mouth wide. His mouth felt numb, and his teeth were sensitive. He didn't feel like it was his body. It was as if all the fear and dread had filtered away, leaving a more positive Joseph in its wake. He was trembling and smiling at the same time. He began to calm and compose himself. His breathing settled and the wishy-washy effect in his head subsided.

Everything still looked the same as before. But it wasn't somehow.

'What am I supposed to do here?' he questioned, the rush of euphoria quickly diminishing and in its place doubt.

'I wanna go home,' he shouted, his voice soon swallowed up by the wind. The next moment he felt the ground ripple underfoot, luckily he was still holding onto the rock. Adding to this, in the distance there were some muffled explosions. What was going on? The youngster instinctively dived on to the chalky ground and scrambled behind a small rock formation. His gaming skills were kicking in. He slipped his facemask over his eyes and mouth, as a cloud of dust gusted towards him. The mini sand storm clouded his visor, obscuring his vision. The ground shook again, loosening slurries of debris from the surrounding rock piles. He felt scared, but a different fear. Joseph felt his chest thump hard with every heartbeat. He had the urge to cry again, but bit back the tears. No, he wasn't going to break down now. Even though he was alone, and in a strange place. Was he in a war-like situation? He needed to find help, maybe the police? His parents would be getting worried by now too. He lay crouched on the ground like some sort of sniper – totally not knowing what to do. Panic again washed over him like an ocean wave. He was trembling, and sweat dripped from his brow. What was he going to do? He tried to focus.

Besides the explosions that were erupting in the distance – there was something else he needed to do, and soon found out.

When he strained his eyes he noticed that his goggles doubled as binoculars. The dust was dissipating now, and he found he could zoom in and out with just his eyes focusing, opening up the complete picture.

'Oh, wow, this is cool,' he gushed. This began to feel more natural. Not only that but, there was data appearing on the right of his vision. This was really James Bond territory. He quickly understood that to get the full data, all he needed to do was a quick flick of his eyes, just to take in the digital listings!

Joseph slowly rotated his head, instead of flinching like some kind of frightened bird. It wasn't long before he could work the equipment as part of his normal eye movements. The data informed him of the distances in metres and mapping references. The rock formations were laid out like a road map. Coordinates and map display – totally military style, he gushed. There was nothing or no one to be seen in his visor, so what was causing the ground to reverberate? He focused more thoroughly taking in the fine detail.

The rocky landscape was chalky-white, and his new uniform made him blend in perfectly. With all this stuff displaying on his visor – you'd have thought that the screen would be obscuring his sight. But, everything was transparent, and visibility was perfectly fine. It was strange too that he actually understood the layout of the software, as if he'd always used it.

'So Mum telling me off for *playing games* late into the night, wasn't really playing games at all. The war type strategies weren't much different to real life,' he realised.

The wind was dying and Joseph wondered after probing the desert, if he was in the Middle East? But what would he be doing here? Not only that, but, where ever he was, was he actually in a war zone... at this moment? That really scared him. He concentrated.

He noticed that the map on his visor also held a pulsing red spot, which appeared to be hovering over some kind of structure in the middle of all this. Was it his destination perhaps? Is this where he's meant to go?

The small explosions had died down like the swirling wind. Visibility was once more restored. It must be the chemistry of this place – sandstorms every few minutes?

But what had actually taken place? He'd been here about twenty minutes now and still was no wiser as to what was going on.

'Oh well,' Joseph sighed, 'Am I supposed to find this point?' This place is warm at least. He could have ended up somewhere in the Artic. He hated the harsh cold of winter. And this suit is cool and comfortable. Well, he was here and there was nothing he could do about it. Until of course, he knew more of his situation. He clambered to his feet and scanned the whole perimeter. There was no one out there, so what caused the explosions? He rechecked the map coordinates. The flashing red dot that pulsed away was still there. The building, over which it hovered, wasn't visible with the high cliffs obscuring his view. 'This must be the way I have to go,' he said. He was unsure, but for the first time in his life, determined to succeed.

His throat was so dry that he couldn't even build up saliva. He needed water and panic again took hold. He'd only just realised that he was wearing a utility belt – like Batman. A surge of excitement filled him. There were two white containers clipped to each side of his waist. Joseph's face lit up. He reached down and unclipped the one on his right. He shook it, and could hear the liquid swishing around inside. There was a flip-top and he flicked it with his thumb and was about to take a gulp. Joseph then realised that the mouthpiece was still in place. It suddenly retracted, leaving his mouth and nose free. Was it safe to drink? He stopped... it had to be water, right? So, before he drank, he lifted it to his nose. It didn't smell of anything. He peered inside, but there was a filter that blocked him from seeing the liquid itself. Sod it, he thought and took a couple of gulps.

'If I'm gonna die – I'm gonna die,' he said flippantly and tilted his head. The liquid was cold and the most delicious water he'd ever tasted. Whoever had put all this together, had thought of everything.

There didn't seem to be any point in hanging around. The target was waiting and he had to find out what he was doing here, and how he was going to get back home? He secured the top to the bottle and clipped it back onto his belt. He lifted the visor off his face for a moment and placed it back onto his forehead again.

The breeze was hot on his skin, but felt good. He pulled off his right glove and rubbed his chin, cheeks and the bridge of his nose. He breathed in a huge lungful of air. It was time to go. He found pockets on both his hips. He took the other glove off and stuffed the two of them inside. He realised that he couldn't leave the visor on his brow. How would he know where to go, the screen with the map was projected inside the lens?

'I need instructions, really,' he said to himself.

'Make your way to that group of rocks to your right.'

Joseph was stunned and stood rigid, holding his breath. He did a full three-sixty and found no one near.

'Who said that?' He was startled. 'Come on, show yourself. Who are you?' Joseph shouted.

'I said it. I am DISC Direct-Interface-Shadow-Control; your on board computer. I can guide you audibly when your visor is not available,' it said.

'My *on board computer* – what, you've been here all along? You've been listening to everything I've been saying? You are built into my visor?' Joseph was outraged.

'Yes, I've been listening to you. But no, I'm not built into your visor. I'm built into your psyche,' DISC said.

'What, you can hear my thoughts?' Joseph screeched getting more agitated by the second.

'Only if you want me to,' DISC relayed with a sombre tone.

'I don't want you to. I don't want you inside my head at all,' Joseph said with a grimace. 'Why didn't you say something to let me know before?' he continued angrily.

'You didn't ask until now,' DISC replied. 'Had you asked me earlier, I would have revealed myself to you.'

'Okay, okay, let's start again, shall we?' Joseph said. At least he had someone to talk to now. 'I don't want you reading my thoughts, for one thing,' Joseph admitted.

'Affirmative,' DISC replied.

'Hi, I am Jos-eph.' He spelled out his name deliberately.

'I have all information needed: You are Joseph Mario Lanes – Male – Fifteen years old. Five-feet-four inches imperial or in metric terms…'

'Okay, okay, I get it, you can stop now. Never mention my middle name again. Do you understand? Never again!' Joseph was adamant. He hated Mario. His father was a Super Mario fan when he was a kid. So he named his son with the hero in mind. Joseph never put his middle name on anything unless he had to. Life was hard enough as it was - he wouldn't just have the twins bullying him, it would be everyone.

'So you're programmed with *all* my information.' Joseph felt intimidated. 'What's your function here, DISC? Why are you here?' he asked.

'To instruct, advise and protect you,' DISC informed.

'Protect. Protect against what? What's out here?' Joseph queried.

'Protect against any dangers that you may encounter,' DISC said simply.

'What dangers might I encounter?' He probed again.

'I do not have that information.'

'All right, advise me, what am I doing here? In fact, where am I exactly? Am I on Earth or the Moon?' Joseph asked sarcastically.

'I do not have that information,' DISC replied.

'You're not much use then are you?' Joseph complained. 'I don't know where I am and what I'm doing here. You are my on board computer with... no information!' Joseph hit back.

'I can instruct and protect,' DISC announced. Joseph shook his head. He knew he wasn't getting any more out of this machine.

'Okay, lead the way to where I'm supposed to go. So where are we going?' Joseph asked again.

'I do not have that…' Joseph cut the computer off before it could continue.

'You do not have that information. I know. Just… take me there,' Joseph groaned, hating DISC more each second.

'Make your way down to that formation of rocks to your right,' DISC instructed once more. Joseph moved off.

'What happens once I get there?' Joseph questioned again.

'I will have more information once we arrive at that destination point.' Joseph now got the impression that this whole thing was pre-programmed. Not just the on board computer, but the whole reason he'd been brought here. Information is being fed to this computer as we go along. Someone is running this whole show, he thought. The answers must be at that location point?

'Okay, DISC, let's move out,' Joseph said, sounding like an army drill sergeant. This brought a smile to his face. Joseph moved off in the direction stipulated by his new friend, and the grumbling seed of doubt bubbled away in his stomach.

Chapter 3

Destination

The sun was bleaching the wide blue vista, as Joseph negotiated the rocks and uneven ground that made up this world. It was quite hard going. He seemed to stumble more than walk.

'I hate this bloody place,' he'd decided after tripping and almost falling on yet another lump of rock. 'Who in their right mind would want to live way out here?' he grumbled again. He was hot and the beads of sweat on his face confirmed that, but inside the suit was reassuringly cool.

'If you would take more time in your walking pattern, Joseph Lanes – then your forward motion would be easier,' DISC instructed.

'I know how to walk, thank you,' he retorted with a sneer. 'You deal with the directions, and I'll deal with the human side of things, okay?' Joseph was feeling irritable and snapped back with anger.

'Affirmative, we are getting to within two kilometres of the target – Joseph Lanes,' DISC assured him.

'DISC - I am Joseph... don't keep adding my last name, it's weird,' Joseph rasped. 'Got it?'

'Joseph... yes, affirmative,' DISC replied. Joseph stopped for a short while to take stock of the situation.

'What am I doing here?'

'You are following my instructions to find the destination you are looking for.' DISC interrupted his half thought.

'DISC, shut up and let me think,' Joseph hissed grinding his teeth, and adding a huff. He was standing just below a small summit. There was a slight breeze, and a puff of dust, which powdered his face, but not enough to constitute putting on his full-face mask. He wasn't that fond of the thing anyway. He wiped his eyes and licked his dry lips – he was thirsty again. He reached to his utility belt and grasped the bottle.

He unclipped the top and eased it to his waiting mouth. It was still cold and he was thankful for that. He swilled it around inside his cheeks – it was pleasant.

'That feels really good,' he said with relief as some spilled out over his lips. He wiped his mouth with the back of his hand and stroked his chin… that's when he heard the cheering. Joseph secured the bottle and quickly replaced it back on his belt. He immediately hit the deck and pulled his visor down. The lens zoomed in on the general direction.

'DISC, what is that?' Joseph asked.

'Am I allowed to speak now?' DISC replied with a flippant tone.

'What? Are you having a tantrum? I thought computers aren't supposed to have hissy fits,' Joseph continued, raising an eyebrow in disbelief.

'Hissy Fit – Tantrum: an emotional outburst usually associated with children – typically characterized by stubbornness and crying. I am not programmed with such human emotions, Joseph – so I can't have a tantrum or a hissy fit,' DISC replied in defence. Joseph didn't carry on with the topic of conversation, and just grinned.

'Yes, DISC, you are allowed to speak now. What is that noise?' Joseph repeated.

'There appears to be a multitude of voices coming from approximately one kilometre north of our position,' DISC informed.

'I have to get a better view,' Joseph said searching the landscape for the best place. He had to get higher and find out exactly what was going on! He looked at the sheer height of the cliffs. That's where I have to go, he thought. The climb would be tricky. The boulders were nestled into the cliff face – sharp and uninviting.

He got to his feet and peeled the mask off his face, then began to scramble upwards – dust and loose shale rolled down behind him. He negotiated the first part easily enough. But there was quite a large rock ahead that he had to get over somehow. It stuck out from the others, awkward and deadly. There were scars dug into the surface of the stone from previous rock falls. Joseph slowly reached up and pushed the fingers of his right hand into a small gap. It felt solid enough, and he reached for a toehold with his right foot. He pushed down and was gaining ground. He felt for another grip with his left foot and hand. All was going well until his right foot shifted slightly, loosening his hold. At that precise moment a gust of wind blew a faceful of grit, which stung his eyes and broke his concentration. He lost his footing altogether and fell straight back off the rock. He tumbled down into a ravine and hit his head when he landed at the bottom, and blacked out!

*

'Joseph-Joseph-Joseph.' He could hear something calling him from far away, but it didn't catch his attention at first. It felt more like a dream, until he sleepily blinked open his eyes. 'You are awake. Vital signs are good.' The sound of DISC's electronic tone seeped through his head. 'You have sustained a slight concussion and some lacerations and bruising, but no major injuries.' The computer concluded, almost sounding happy. The teenager looked through half-opened lids. He waited for the world to slow down.

He was flat on his back – upside-down, and at an angle. His head throbbed immediately when he became aware, and everything else seemed to ache too.

'I h-have to get… up,' he winced, trying to move his legs, loose stones rolling down each side of his torso. All the weight of his body felt as though it was settled on his head and shoulders. He couldn't really move. 'My… mouth is… dry,' he said with a certain amount of strain, sticking out his dry tongue in a bid to make moisture. He remembered the water and slowly reached for the bottle, but to his horror, it wasn't there! He felt so sick. 'Where's my bottle?'

'You have two water bottles, Joseph,' DISC informed him. 'There is also one on your left side.'

'I know, I remember,' Joseph replied, still trying to recover his senses. He felt with his left hand just to make sure. But before he drank it, he decided he needed to roll over. With all the strength he could muster, he lifted his left shoulder and twisted it across his body.

'Aaargh,' he squealed, as the impact he'd sustained revealed itself in a flurry of pain. He got to the point of no return, as his body weight rolled over naturally. He landed on his stomach. This was all too much, with the headache and blood rush, he subsequently threw up.

'You appear to be vomiting.' DISC relayed the obvious. 'The concussion will bring that on.'

Joseph wanted to answer back so badly, but actually couldn't; he was in too much pain and other bodily functions prevented speech. When he'd finished, he managed to push himself away from the mess and got to his knees. It took a while to steady himself, and once he did, things slowly returned to normal. He felt a little better and spat the last of the vomit from his mouth. He grasped the bottle from his hip and took a small sip – swilling out the bad taste. He took slow sips in increments to relieve his thirst, and eased back onto his haunches. His head thumped but that was the least of his problems. He could see the other water bottle, further down, buckled and pierced, the last of the water in a damp patch next to it. That's had it, he thought.

'DISC, how long was I out?' he asked croakily, rolling his shoulders – his back really hurting.

'One hour – seventeen minutes and eight seconds,' DISC reported correctly. Joseph arched his back and twisted his head from side-to-side. It didn't matter which way he moved, everything hurt from top to bottom.

'I have to get back up there,' he said not relishing the climb again.

'You must take care this time,' DISC said pointlessly.

'Are you for real?' Joseph said shaking his head in disbelief.

'Oh yes, Joseph, I am for real. And if I don't instruct you properly, you could harm yourself again.'

'I-I... what?' Joseph couldn't find anything of substance to answer with, so didn't bother. He realised that he hadn't fallen that far and the channel he'd fallen into – reached right to the top. It also held smaller rocks that would be easier to climb, and a lot safer – which would please DISC. Joseph, at least, chuckled at that thought.

'Okay, here goes,' he willed himself. It was a difficult ascent, but not as bad as the other way. He stopped midway up and took another sip of water. He continued climbing and soon found himself over the ridge and standing at the peak. The wind was stronger up here, and he felt it whipping around his body. He gazed down into the next valley and took in the enormity of the desert. He slipped his goggles back on. It didn't take him long to find what he was looking for. There it was right in front of him. The automatic lens zoomed in to reveal a building. It was as white as the background. The structure was also huge, resembling an arena! It looked from here to be the same size as a large football stadium. The sounds he'd been following were coming from there. His vision though only just reached the open rooftop. There was definite movement inside, but he couldn't pinpoint anything particular. The red dot on his monitor was flashing away dead centre.

'We found it, DISC?' he said simply.

'That is your destination, Joseph,' DISC's voice informed him, crackling through his earpiece.

What is in there that is so important? It was a total mystery. He was just an ordinary schoolboy. What was so special about him that they needed him here?

Joseph looked down the slope and further to the bottom. There were the usual loose stones and rocks and he didn't relish another fall. He made his way down in a zigzag manoeuvre, taking away the steep angle of the mountain. It was again hard going, and listening to titbits of information, stating the obvious, from DISC made it even harder.

By the time Joseph got to the bottom he'd created a small dust cloud from the disturbance. He stood silent. He was standing at the base of a canyon. Now, all he had to do was walk a little bit further – through a gap in the two gigantic boulders, and soon he would be there. He didn't know what he had to do once he'd arrive, but that was something else to sort later.

The air cleared, so he lifted off the goggles and placed them on his forehead again.

To be fair he hadn't been wearing them for that long, but the freedom when they were off was welcoming. He remembered when he started swimming lessons at six, and had to wear those horrible goggles in the water. The elastic twisted around his hair – trapping and pulling at his roots. Also the eyecups sucked into his sockets and nearly pulled out his eyeballs. He stopped thinking about the past for a second, when a strange sound caught his train of thought.

Joseph rubbed his eyes and dipped his breathing levels to a shallow pant. There it was again – a strange sound coming from above. A deep rumbling, almost a purr. Some debris rolled down and landed at his feet. He needed to look up and see what had caused it, but he was too afraid. I don't need any more adventures, he thought.

There was a long earthy growl, which vibrated through the rocks and up through his body. This brought a sense of fear.

'Crap.' Joseph stood rigid. Then, with all the courage he could muster, he slowly, and without any sudden movements, raised his sights. His eyes would have fallen out if he'd opened them any wider. He immediately slipped his goggles back over his eyes.

'Oh my God,' he said with a tremble. He swallowed hard. 'A tiger – yeah, definitely a tiger of sorts.' But to make things worse, if that were possible, it had tusks, jutting up from its bottom jaw. The cat was huge, at least the length of a car and a half. The strange thing was, it didn't have stripes. It had a full body of yellow fur and added to that, long floppy ears. It was standing majestically on a large column of rocks, high above, as if asserting its domain. Its large green eyes were transfixed directly on Joseph's.

'A sabre-toothed tiger... b-but that's impossible,' he stammered. The last time he'd seen anything like it was in the movie *Ice Age*. 'T-take it easy, girl,' he felt himself mumble. 'I'm not going to harm you.' Who am I kidding, he thought. The beast was readying itself to leap down on him. Joseph didn't know what to do.

'When it jumps, Joseph – you must leap out of the way, onto the ridge to your left,' DISC informed him with cool succinct instructions. 'Ready yourself.'

The tiger, without warning, leapt off the column and came down, silently cutting through the air. Joseph didn't think anymore and ran. The tiger had landed perfectly with a slight thud, and immediately righted itself. Now it was headed straight for him!

'You must jump out of harm's way, Joseph, or it will tear you to pieces,' DISC instructed urgently.

'B-but, I can't jump that high,' Joseph stuttered. 'It's too far up.'

'Don't think... just do it,' DISC insisted. The tiger was almost on him. Joseph didn't have any time to react – he squeezed his eyes shut while pushing off the ground.

'You can open your eyes now, Joseph. You've done it.' DISC sounded pleased, if a robotic voice can. Joseph opened his eyes. He was standing on the ledge, facing inwards. He turned and realised that he'd sprung about nine metres.

'Wha... how did I do that?' He had no time to question himself – the tiger was already sprinting towards him. There was an incline just behind and the agile tiger was almost at the top.

'Stand your ground, Joseph,' DISC commanded. 'You have the capability to defeat this animal.'

'Are you messing with me?' Joseph said. 'It's a bloody tiger, for God's sake.' The tiger's approach was instant. Joseph immediately jumped off the ledge and flew through the air. He landed on the rock tower that the tiger had leapt from in the first place. He spun around, still reeling from the amazing feat he'd just done. The tiger though was right behind him.

'You have to defend yourself, Joseph,' DISC insisted.

'I-I can't... it's too big!' Joseph raged.

'No, it's not,' DISC reiterated. 'You can defeat this beast.'

Joseph again jumped off the high rock and almost floated down from the great height, and onto the ground. But the tiger was right there with him. Joseph didn't have time to regain his senses and escape. The tiger lashed out with its right paw and the impact knocked him flying across the ground.

'Defend yourself, Joseph, or this animal will kill you here and now.' DISC continued belching instructions.

Disorientated, Joseph got up, but was faced with a mini sand blizzard. 'Where did that come from?' he gulped. The sensors in his visor were knocked offline. For the first time in a long while, he felt helpless!

The grainy image of swirling sand obliterated everything on his screen.

'Where the hell is the tiger?' he screamed, but the wind and grit had also taken DISC. He was truly alone. 'What is that?' Joseph could see a dark shape in the ever-changing storm. He tensed. The shadow manifested itself into human forms. Joseph began to gag. He couldn't believe that his mum and dad were standing there. His mouth quivered and tears escaped the corners of his eyes.

It didn't take long before the figures faded and Joseph could feel himself reaching out for them – a lump welling in his throat. Then another set of shapes emerged of two more people – a man and a woman. Joseph was strangely attracted to them, as if he knew them, but didn't recognise them, he couldn't understand it. They quickly dissolved and the tiger leapt straight through their image! But, strangely enough, Joseph was now ready and didn't flinch!

There was a ton of animal trying to kill him and he was, for once, in control. He quickly lifted his arm, and flicked his hand to the right, and an invisible force emanated from his fingers. The feeling of power was overwhelming, he'd never felt this way before.

The tiger twisted like a corkscrew in mid-flight, and was flung like a discarded drinks carton. It yelped as it crashed into a pile of rocks, that ripped a gash in its side, blood pouring from it. The sandstorm dissipated as quickly as it came, and vision was again restored.

The poor beast, for the first time, looked startled. It shook its enormous head and re-focussed. It spotted Joseph again and lifted itself back onto its four legs, a little wobbly at first. Once it had asserted itself, it came limping towards him in another half-hearted attack. But this was a different Joseph now. This new wise teenager was totally ready. He swiftly dived out of its way. It lashed out and missed, tumbling into a heap, yelping and bleating. The anger was clear as its green eyes flared. It raised itself once more and surged forwards with everything it had. Joseph sprang into the air and flipped over the top of it, landing on his feet behind. The tiger couldn't stop and cracked its head on the rocks. There was a cloud of dust, as it tried to regain its senses.

It turned and burst through the grey and came at him once more! Without any fear or nerves, Joseph sprang from his position and landed high on the ridge above. The tiger was still lunging forward, not really sure where Joseph had gone. It stopped, and shook its head. It growled a loud resounding snarl that echoed up through the ravine. Joseph simply dropped down and planted his whole body weight right at the back of the tiger's head. Its jaw came crunching down under the immense pressure.

By this time Joseph had flipped off and landed safely in front of it. He stood, chest heaving, wondering what went on in the last three minutes? Was DISC giving him the instructions or was he doing all this himself? The tiger looked at Joseph and clambered upright. The creature dropped its head and padded over to the teenager, rubbing its body against his side. Joseph was blown away. Did all this just happen?

'I've completely defeated a tiger! Brilliant! A sabre-tooth bloody tiger!' he exclaimed. He looked up and couldn't believe he'd leapt from the ridge. But he'd landed with no effort.

'DISC is back online,' DISC reported.

'DISC, who the hell have I turned into? What have you done to me?' he cried.

'I have done nothing. It's all inside you, Joseph,' DISC admitted. 'I was offline for five minutes and forty-two seconds, Joseph. I have no memory of that time.'

'But none of this came about until I put that disc on my chest,' Joseph remembered. 'I wouldn't have even got here if it wasn't for that thing.'

'It's time to go to the arena, Joseph. I'm sure the answers you are looking for are there,' DISC retorted.

'I think you're right, DISC. Come on, let's go.' He was about to move off when he peered into the tiger's large, green eyes. "You can't come with us," Joseph said. "You'll have to run along. Off you go." He shooed the creature away and watched it disappear into the distance with a sadness pulling at his heart.

Chapter 4

The Others

Joseph dusted himself down – puffs of grey lifted from the material of his suit. He eased the goggles on to his forehead and felt the hot air on his sweaty face. He didn't really need to use his goggles now – he knew where the arena was situated. He took a swig from his bottle and walked along the path that divided the parallel rocks. He could visually see the building ahead. It wasn't that far away from his present position. He stopped while he took in the view from ground level.

'What do you think, DISC?' Joseph asked, still trying to get used to... everything!

'What do I think of what Joseph, you'll have to be more specific?' DISC responded. Joseph scratched his cheek, wondering why he bothered to ask the opinion of his computer at all sometimes.

'What do you think about the situation I'm in?' Joseph questioned feeling a little frustrated.

'I don't understand – the situation is, you have to find out what your journey is all about,' the computer countered. 'It's self-explanatory.'

'I know that... what do you think about that?' He pointed ahead towards the arena.

'I cannot give any more information until I encounter more data,' DISC replied ominously.

'You're useless, DISC,' Joseph grunted.

'I can perform millions of calculations in a micro second, Joseph. I am useful, not useless,' DISC reminded him.

'Mmmm, you sound annoyed,' Joseph grinned.

'Impossible, I cannot be annoyed, agitated, frustrated…'

'Okay, okay, I get the picture. Sorry I even asked,' Joseph said as he continued on. 'Now shut up.'

The building was a colossal white affair, and blended into the background of the desert seamlessly. He tried to get more clarity, some extra information, but it was too bright. So he placed the goggles back over his eyes. He focused and the picture amplified in greater detail.

'These goggles are great, DISC,' he uttered, 'even if they do take a little getting used to.'

'It's good you like them,' DISC replied, nonplussed. 'They are useful and decorative.'

Joseph wasn't quite sure about the last part. 'Can computers sound bored, because you do?' Joseph added sarcastically.

'Computers are not programmed with attitudes, Joseph,' DISC said, really sounding as if he did. They continued walking towards the open spaces and left behind the rock laden landscape. The sun beat down on him, like a lead weight.

As he approached the structure, there didn't seem to be much activity outside the walls, but he could hear chanting and cheering as the wind gusted in his direction. The closer he got, the realisation and enormity of the building, truly took hold. It dwarfed everything around it. There was a large grand entrance, which depicted an arch hewn from solid rock. Joseph stopped and studied the artwork. There were patterns and figures carved skilfully into the surface of the façade. He took a closer look, but couldn't make any sense of the design.

'I don't recognise any of this, DISC,' he said. Maybe if he did recognise something, it could give him a clue as to why he'd been brought here, he thought.

'I can't help you I'm afraid, Joseph. From here on in, you have to find your own path,' DISC said with a hint of finality. Joseph felt a slight shudder through his body, and a release of sorts. He shrugged it off not knowing what it meant.

There were no gates here, the entrance was fully open, and that's where he made for. He stood at the edge of the opening. In front of him, and painted into the floor was a thin blue line. The line itself was the thickness of a ribbon, the kind of ribbon depicting the end of a racing event.

'Well, here goes, DISC,' Joseph said and stepped over. 'I'm in, DISC.' He waited for an answer. 'DISC, I'm in.' But his computer didn't reply. No matter how much he called out, it was gone. He was on his own again and that was a huge drop in confidence.

The corridor swept uphill and narrowed at the end. The sound of thousands of voices was at its highest point. Joseph tentatively moved forward and realised there was a gate further up. He approached and saw someone sitting inside. It resembled a ticket office! This was even weirder than the experience in the desert. He strolled near the window, which only revealed the head and arms of the occupier. The glass was dirty with an open section at the counter. The person inside was a man in his fifties, semi-bald with a thick moustache, like Mr Browns, Joseph's history teacher.

'Come on, hurry up,' the man rasped, his voice muffled by the partition. He stuck out his hand, which was clenched around a wooden stamp. Joseph looked at his hairy, chubby fingers. The man waited anxiously. Joseph lifted his arm, looked at his hand and placed his palm facedown, on the counter. It was over before he realised. The back of his hand now had: Access, stamped on it in bold lettering – then the ink faded away. Joseph stared curiously as the last of the impression disappeared. He peered back at the glass.

'Go on inside quickly,' the ticket master said bluntly.

'Where do I go?' Joseph looked bewildered.

'Don't dawdle, young man, move along,' the man insisted.

'B-but...' Joseph wasn't given time to ask anything else.

'Look, don't hang around, go inside quickly,' the ticket master continued. 'You don't want to lose your place, do you?' he said and slammed down the shutter.

'Lose what place? What are you talking about? Hey,' Joseph shouted and slapped on the glass, but it was useless. The man had disappeared. Joseph stood silent, and didn't know why he had to go inside. He pushed the bar and it clicked as he walked through. Soon he was ushered by someone else. This person was tall and silent, with no expression. He escorted Joseph to a large white door. Joseph stood waiting, totally disorientated, and feeling out of place.

*

The ball bounced past the goal post and into the nearby bushes. Steve Green went sprinting after it.

'Damn it, my penalties are shocking,' he mumbled as he rummaged around in the undergrowth. 'Where the hell is it?' Steve was the newest recruit of the school football team. He needed to sharpen up on heading and penalties – his tackling was pretty good, his coach had told him.

Steve was the only one in the park at the time; he wanted to be on his own. He needed to practise without anyone from his team seeing him. He didn't need another bout of ribbing from his so called teammates. Steve was tall and thin, and held a head of bushy brown hair.

'Where is that bloody ball?' he cursed; patience was not his strongest virtue. The sun on the field had bleached his eyesight. It took a while to adjust, going from blinding white to black shadow in a split-second. It was one of those hot days when the heat sapped your energy. 'Ah, there you are,' he said and stooped down to pick it up. By now his eyes were more accustomed to the shade. He did have that annoying red blob dancing around in front of his vision, but there was something else here too, that pushed through the blurriness.

There was some kind of light pulsing away in the thicket. He threw the ball out into the thin grass and turned back. It was still there – a green light cutting through the fading red haze. He reached in and brushed away the overhang of vines and grass, making sure there were no nettles; he'd got an annoying rash last time.

'That's weird,' he said to himself, getting more excited by the second. He lifted it out, pulling away at the stubborn tangle of greenery. 'Let go, you cow,' he cursed. 'Oh, it's a disc,' he said, looking a bit put out, he was hoping for something more exciting. He looked to see if anyone had strolled by, that he hadn't noticed. There wasn't, he was all on his own. He rubbed his chin in thought. 'It's been here a while by the look of things,' he continued to reason with himself. 'Can't belong to anyone, there's no one here.' He studied it for a short while. It was kind of metallic and round, with a throbbing green light at its centre. The pulsing light was hypnotic and he felt the urge to touch it. And he did!

*

Joseph saw that the white door was opening, sliding to one side. He turned to the person who'd led him there to ask a question, but was shoved inside before he'd had a chance to utter anything.

'Hey, take it easy,' Joseph protested, but was met with no response. The door swished shut and he immediately turned to grab the handle, but there wasn't one. He smacked his hand hard on the smooth surface – it stung with every hit. 'Hey, what's happening? You can't lock me in here – I can call Child Line and report you. Let me out you creep?' Joseph cried, vigorously rubbing and blowing his wringing palm. The room was white just like the rest of the building, and he was alone in there. There were benches fixed to the walls, like a changing room, but no windows. This felt like being inside a very clinical prison. What is it with this whole white decor thing, he thought.

'What's happening? Why am I in here? I haven't done anything wrong,' he shouted in desperation, and when no one answered, he slumped down on the nearest bench. He leaned

over and dropped his head into his hands, resting h.
his knees. He'd never felt so solitary, and even ı
attention of the McKenzie brothers. He ran that over in
once more and thought better of it.

'Oh God, can things get any worse?' he moaned.

Then something amazingly strange happened, as if things
weren't strange enough already! Figures began to appear from
nowhere, right in front of him, and stood in the middle of the
room. Joseph pressed his back against the wall and watched in
silence, his heart rate quickening.

Firstly, a girl appeared – then a boy, and then another girl,
and finally a second boy. No one knew what to say. They were
all dressed in the same white uniform as he wore. They also had
the goggle mask on top of their heads. The two girls were slim
and roughly medium height. Quite hot too, he thought. One had
short brown hair, while the other – long blonde hair tied in a
ponytail. The two boys stood confused, one tall with a thin
frame and bushy hair, looked a bit like a stick of celery. The
other boy, was much shorter and robust, wearing specs and a
short cropped hairstyle. Once they'd all fully materialised, they
stepped away from the centre of the room. The four of them
appeared dishevelled, as he did. They didn't know each other,
which was obvious to Joseph, especially as they didn't want to
be near one another. The next few minutes there was a lot of
confusion and edginess between the group. Finally, the tall boy
spoke.

'What am I doing here?' he snapped, the anger apparent.

'Yeah, what's going on?' the shorter one added, looking
equally confused.

'I asked first,' the first boy rounded.

'So, is that supposed to intimidate me?' the shorter of the two hit back. There was a stand-off. Then one of the girls spoke, which broke the moment.

'What am I wearing?' the girl in the ponytail asked, and was quietly admiring herself, until she'd realised that the other girl was wearing the same clothes.

'Same here, but not following her obviously,' the other girl chirped in, half pointing to the girl opposite. They were so caught up in the situation that they hadn't noticed Joseph sitting there. He felt compelled to speak.

'Hi,' Joseph said from behind, lifting his right hand into the air in a greeting. They all turned in his direction.

'Who are you?' the short boy probed, with eyes squinting, looking really intense.

'I-I'm Joseph ... Joseph Lanes,' Joseph replied meekly, feeling a little bit intimidated.

'What am I doing here?' the tall one repeated, lifting his arms to check out his outfit.

'Same question?' the smaller boy said also, eyeing the suit on his round body.

'I'm asking the question, dumpy,' the taller of the two interrupted, rudely.

'Would you like me to dump you, Mr Tall?' the smaller boy challenged.

'Yeah, come on...' But the tall one didn't have a chance to continue.

'Now now, boys, play fair, or I'll take your toys away – toys being Mr Men figures, obviously,' the girl with the ponytail cut in sharply, grinning.

'Shut it, princess,' the tall boy growled, his face filled with rage.

'Whooo, hit a nerve have I?' Ponytail rebounded.

'Your social skills are nil, my friend,' the shorter boy retaliated. The tall boy calmed, and took a few breaths. This gave everyone a moment to collect his or her thoughts.

'Hi, Joseph, I'm Sarah Grim,' the girl with the bob said sweetly. She was nice. Joseph liked her more than Miss Ponytail at this point. He smiled at her and she gave him a quirky look back in return, whilst wrinkling her nose.

'Jenna Tranter, which I suppose I should have said initially, but I'm... really confused,' the ponytailed girl said.

'Keiron Evans,' the smaller boy spoke, his specs glinting in the white room.

'Steve Green,' the tall boy added, peering at his surroundings.

'Well now we've introduced ourselves, does anyone know why we're here? Wherever here is?' Jenna enquired.

Joseph sat, shaking his head.

'What about you, Joe?' Keiron looked at him with wide expectant eyes. 'You look as though you were here before us?'

'I've no idea either. I've made my way here from outside,' Joseph admitted. There was a collective agreement from the others.

'You came through the desert too?' Jenna asked.

'I did, but I'm not sure how, it was crazy out there,' Joseph admitted.

'Yeah, scary,' Jenna replied.

'Where is that noise coming from? I didn't get to see anyone when I arrived,' Sarah said remembering the din in the background.

'I think we're in some kind of a stadium,' Joseph explained. 'It's what it looked and felt like coming here.'

'I agree,' Steve said, thinking of his experience.

'Yeah, like a huge football ground,' Keiron added.

'The O2 but a totally different shape,' Jenna said, comparing in her head.

'Does this mean we're in some kind of competition?' Steve said curiously, 'especially as we're in these stupid jump suits. What are we competing for?'

'There's only one way to find out, we have to get out of here,' Keiron insisted. Jenna walked to the door, but there wasn't a button to press or any indication as to how it opened.

'This is stupid. How do we get out of here?' Jenna screeched. 'I have to get home.' Her more vulnerable side began to show.

'They can't keep us prisoner here,' Sarah sympathised. 'We should try to contact the police.'

'Err, that may be difficult,' Joseph said pursing his lips together. 'I don't think we're on… Earth,' he said and wished he hadn't.

'What do you mean you don't think we're on Earth? That's ridiculous. Don't be so stupid,' Steve said with a grimace. 'Where the hell do you think we are, then? On the Moon?'

'I'm telling you, from what I've seen, outside doesn't look anything like where I'm from. It's desert and rock and doesn't feel like our… planet!'

'Explain, Joe?' Keiron asked calmly.

'I-err... saw a... sabre-toothed tiger!' he blurted out. There was total silence. Eyes were rolling from person to person.

'A sabre-toothed tiger?' Jenna said with a puff.

'Are you serious?' Steve was grinning and shaking his head.

'You don't know me, and I don't know you. But, I've no reason to lie,' Joseph reacted smartly.

'What happened to it?' Sarah asked with interest.

'I-I... I hid from it,' Joseph lied, thinking to himself, did it really take place? 'And it ran off.'

'Oh, sounds scary,' Sarah said, not looking fully convinced.

'Sounds completely rubbish to me,' Steve added.

Joseph didn't answer.

'Let's be honest, can anyone else explain where we are, or what we're doing here?' Keiron asked. 'I'm inclined to believe Joseph.'

'Come on,' Steve retorted. 'Really?'

'Well, there's something weird about this place, you've got to admit that,' Keiron said.

'If we are on a different planet – how can we breathe?' Jenna queried.

'I don't have any of the answers,' Joseph shrugged his shoulders. 'I'm as mystified as you lot.'

'This can't be happening,' Sarah piped up. 'I have to get home too.'

'Why would you say we aren't on Earth?' Steve quizzed. 'Besides the sabre-toothed story?'

Joseph felt angry for once, and got it straight in his head. 'You all had an on board computer?' Joseph questioned. 'It's called DISC and came online when the discs that got you here magnetized to your chests?'

There was a collective nod of heads.

'Yeah, but it doesn't answer anymore,' Keiron uttered. 'It shut off after I got my hand stamped by that creepy ticket guy.'

'Me too,' said Jenna.

'Yeah,' Steve nodded again.

'Same thing,' Sarah agreed.

'Did DISC get you here, though?' Joseph questioned.

'Yeah, so what?' Steve said. 'It gave me a map and instructions, but that was it.'

'Did you all feel different when the discs magnetized to you?' Joseph continued.

'Yes, I felt a sense of adrenalin kick in,' Keiron immediately realised, nodding, but in his eyes you could see he was working things out.

'Yeah, me too,' Steve admitted and narrowed his eyes sceptically.

'Yeah, same here,' Jenna said with a wide grin.

'Ditto,' Sarah agreed.

'I'd felt that when I'd first arrived,' Joseph admitted. 'But did you also notice that you could do things that you couldn't do before?'

'Such as?' Steve was intrigued. 'I only felt different. What kinds of things?'

'Running faster, jumping higher, improved vision and hearing – you name it, even… flying! Everything was better than before, and other things that I couldn't do, now I can,' Joseph told them, the excitement building inside.

'Yeah, right,' Keiron said sceptically. 'Flying?'

'No, honestly, I could do incredible things out there,' Joseph said.

'Show us then?' Steve insisted. 'Fly. You said you could, do it!'

'Oh, okay,' Joseph replied reluctantly, hoping that the loss of DISC wouldn't be the loss of his powers. 'You want me to… fly?' He swallowed hard. 'I'll fly.'

'I'd like to see that!' Keiron pressed. 'Can you do it right now?'

'I honestly don't know the answer to that,' Joseph admitted.

'So you can't then?' Steve said flippantly.

'Well, with DISC gone… okay then, here goes,' he said and stood up. The others made a circle around him, but stepped back a safe distance. Joseph took a deep breath, lifted his arms and then, without warning, the white door slid open!

Chapter 5

Zaan

Joseph stopped what he was about to do, and the other four teenagers hushed and waited to see who or what was entering the room. They didn't have to wait long as in walked a tall, slim person – in a black and white suit. The suit held no lapels or pockets and the black stripes contrasted with the bleach white of the room.

The person, who looked mostly human, had short-cropped hair, which was greasily pasted flat to his small, round head. He looked at them, his eyes wide apart and immersed in a milky residue. His nose was almost flat to his face, with a thin mouth, like a zipper bag. He smiled an untrustworthy grin and seemed to glide over the threshold. He stood silently at first, and peered at the five bemused youngsters. The door shut silently behind him. He sensed when the door was closed and opened his mouth to speak.

'Please sit,' he said in a soft tone, which felt more like an order rather than a request. No one moved, intrigued as to what was going to happen next. The man widened his stare, furrowed his brow and nodded towards the seating area. He gestured with his right hand.

'Please,' he insisted, but not raising his voice. This seemed to do the trick and they joined Joseph as he sat back on the bench. 'You are all probably wondering what is happening, and what you are doing here. Am I right?' He scanned his audience. There were empty nods all around. The man stroked his round chin thoughtfully.

Then Joseph broke the silence, which for him was a milestone. 'Y-yes, actually I... Err, we were.' The words tumbled out awkwardly from his mouth.

'Yeah, what's going on, mate?' Steve was more sharp and direct.

'I want to know what's happening too?' Keiron also added.

'Me too,' Jenna said and nodded. Sarah didn't speak – she only shook her head in compliance with the others.

'I can totally understand that you are probably feeling scared, confused and annoyed at being brought here. Let me introduce myself; my name is Zaan.' The man said the words with an air of importance, and pushed out his chest. There was grinning from all five, but no one said anything. 'And if you listen to what I have to say, I can explain everything you need to know.' Keiron was about to speak again, when Zaan put his finger to his lips. 'Listen,' he said and squinted to reinforce his command. Keiron grimaced, but said no more.

'Everything I'm about to tell you is true. So let me finish before bombarding me with questions. Would that be all right?' He took a breath and everyone nodded. 'I know all about you. You are all orphans, am I correct?' Zaan looked at his audience again. He waited, but no one answered even though each pair of eyes told a different story. 'Oh, of course you can speak to answer me,' he said with an amused giggle. They all looked at one another and whispered, all to the annoyance of Zaan. They spoke silently and ushered Steve to answer for them.

'Yes, we are all orphans,' Steve finally spoke up, and added, 'how did you know?' Zaan paused and smoothed a finger over each eyebrow, keeping them perfectly flattened.

'Your names are, Joseph Lanes, Jenna Tranter, Sarah Grim, Steve Green and Keiron Evans. Is that correct? Just nod,' Zaan insisted. They did, but all looked deadly shocked and astounded. 'This world we are all in right now is called Ether World – you are not on Earth. When you were all first born you were taken from here and placed on Earth.' This sent a shiver of fear right through all of them.

'You're crazy, you—' Jenna was about to speak when she was immediately cut off, with Zaan raising his hand again to stop her.

'Please do not interrupt, I'll take questions later,' he said with a sharp look of distaste. 'You were placed on Earth for a very good reason, and that was to learn Earth ways. Your mission was to pick up all the information you could, and once you reached fifteen, were to be returned to Ether World. Now you have been brought back to us. You will be trained in the art of combat – the Etherian way. This will take place easily from DISC, the on board intelligence system that you are wearing,' Zaan explained.

'Hold on…' Joseph tried to interrupt, but was dismissed by Zaan too.

'D-I-S-C,' he pronounced each of the exact lettering. 'Direct-Interface-Shadow-Control. The discs are an intelligent entity, unlike its hosts,' he added flippantly. 'Its job,' he continued, 'is to connect with your minds. Each individual voice, gives instructions on how to proceed. The skills you need are deep within yourselves and the disc will find and enhance them. Then, when you are prepared, you can go back to Earth,' he said. 'Now, you may ask me any questions.'

'Trained for combat, are you mad?' Jenna spoke first. 'I'm not training for anything. I'm not a soldier – I'm a schoolgirl,' she said defiantly, instantly regretting the schoolgirl bit.

'We're not at war with anyone, and we're too young to fight anyway,' Sarah added.

'You are at war or will be with Earth,' Zaan stated, for the first time showing his anger.

'So you're telling us, w-we're not human and we have to fight against Earth?' Jenna said with a tremble. 'I-I can't take this in.'

'Yes, that is correct.' Zaan closed his eyes in contempt. 'You are definitely Etherians. Don't you ever listen?' he replied sharply.

'B-but my mum and dad,' Jenna gasped.

'They're not your parents. You knew that you were orphans anyway,' Zaan countered, and seemed to enjoy the reaction.

'I know they're not my parents,' Jenna snapped back, 'b-but they're all I've ever known. You're telling me I'm an alien?'

'If we're all aliens, why haven't we got milky eyes like you?' Sarah questioned.

'Yeah, explain that?' Steve said in compliance.

'You were all put on Earth fifteen years ago. Your eyes have adapted to Earth's atmosphere. I noticed that when I arrived. You were put there to evolve and one day come back home. You're not aliens. You are originally from this world. Your Earth parents are the aliens,' Zaan responded.

'You're talking rubbish,' Jenna said tearfully, 'I haven't travelled in any ship, how can I be on a different planet? You're nuts.'

'Look, hold on...' Zaan tried to keep the conversation in some kind of context, but was being pulled from every angle.

'Yeah, this is stupid. I don't believe a word of it,' Steve grunted. 'Aliens, come on? Let us out of here now. You can't keep us locked up in here,' Steve insisted and stood up, followed by the others, except for Joseph.

'Wait a minute...' but Zaan couldn't keep control.

'I don't believe any of this either, it's a bunch of crap,' Keiron responded bearing his teeth, face screwed in anger. Steve ran at the door. He kicked and clawed, trying to get it open. The others joined him, but it was no use.

'SIT DOWN!' Zaan commanded, but raising his voice didn't help. Steve and Keiron turned towards him. The glare in their eyes was of horror and confusion. They shifted a look at one another and seemed to send a signal.

'Open this door, mate?' Steve spat angrily. 'Open it now!'

'Yeah, open the door?' Keiron said, his temper rising. At this point Joseph stood up.

'You can't keep us here,' Joseph said adamantly and joined in with the others. Quickly things got out of control. Keiron and Steve could take no more and charged at Zaan head on. He didn't flinch, standing his ground. They sped towards him but hadn't made it halfway across the room, when Zaan calmly raised his right hand. The charge was instantly halted, and the two boys were frozen where they stood, like pausing a digital channel on television. Joseph, Jenna and Sarah looked on in disbelief. Silence once more engulfed the room.

Then Jenna spoke up. 'What have you done?' She was astonished.

Sarah and Joseph couldn't take in what was happening either. The even stranger thing was, that their eyes were manically moving around inside their heads. You could tell just from that - that they were in distress, even though their bodies weren't moving.

'Everyone calm down.' Zaan returned to his smooth velvety voice.

'P-please, let them go,' Jenna pleaded. 'You're hurting them.'

'They aren't hurt, just annoyed and frustrated, probably.' Zaan flicked his eyelids and lowered his hand. The boys flopped to the floor, as if thawed from a freezer. It took some time to catch their breath and compose themselves again.

'You sure you haven't hurt them?' Sarah complained, 'they look pretty upset to me.'

'They're fine,' Zaan retorted flippantly, 'it was just a momentary stasis.' They came around quickly and got to their feet, still disorientated.

'What are you?' Keiron said, still trying to focus and also feeling wobbly.

'What did you just do to us?' Steve questioned, chest heaving.

'Now do you believe me?' he said smartly. 'Could I have done that if I were on Earth?'

'I don't know what I believe anymore,' Joseph said honestly.

'Right, let's try this again shall we?' Zaan continued. 'I know this is a lot to take in, but it is all true. You are originally from here, and here is Ether World. You also all have powers.

Wasn't Joseph just about to show you, before I entered the room?'

'You know?' Joseph looked surprised.

'Of course I know. I know everything that goes on here,' he said with a grin.

'Yes, you were about to show us, weren't you?' Steve chipped in.

'I know Joseph can do it. So now, Keiron, it's your turn. I want you to jump,' Zaan said. 'Just jump and see how high you can go. See if you can touch say, way up there.' Keiron looked up. The domed ceiling was a good nine metres high.

'I can't jump that high it's impossible, you're crazy,' Keiron gasped gawking upwards.

'If you're human you can't, but if you're Etherian, then it won't be a problem… will it?' Zaan insisted.

'You're saying we can all do this?' Jenna asked.

'See what Keiron does first,' Zaan said, casting her a passing glance.

'Right, okay then, I will. But this is bloody stupid. I need a trampoline or something,' Keiron said, mumbling to himself. 'I'll have to take off this body armour,' he insisted, 'it'll hold me down.'

'The armour is light and won't hinder you in the slightest. Besides, you can't take it off in a battle situation,' Zaan added.

'There you go with that again. I'm not fighting anyone, mate,' Steve insisted, 'I've still got my A levels to do.'

'Me neither,' added Joseph.

Keiron didn't join in; he was concentrating on his task.

'Look, let's just see what Keiron does first and then we can go into that later,' Zaan said trying to move the conversation away from war for the moment.

Keiron walked to the middle of the room – the ceiling was at its highest point. The sheer vastness of the area made it all the more daunting. Everyone waited with interest. Keiron studied the distance from his position and swallowed hard. He peered back at his new friends – they urged him on. Joseph knew he could do it. He'd already done it himself and realised how scary it felt. Keiron took off his glasses and gestured for Joseph to come forward to take them.

'You can do this,' Joseph whispered in his ear.

'If you say so,' he replied nervously. Keiron bent his knees and leaned forward, taking a deep breath before he pushed off. He sprang! He could feel the air push against his face and his body didn't feel real. There were gasps from below, but he didn't have time to look down. It all happened so quickly and he literally had to push out his hands to protect his face from the interior ceiling. He banged straight into the surface and everything spun around and around. The sudden impact engulfed his senses and his concentration dissolved. Soon he was heading straight back down to the ground. He landed with a resounding thud! Zaan smirked and everyone else was gobsmacked.

They all rushed over to see if he was all right.

Joseph got there first and flipped him over onto his back. 'Keiron? Keiron, are you okay?' he shouted, with concern plastered all over his face.

Keiron lay still with a huge stupid smile on his chubby face. He sucked in air and breathed as if it was a new commodity.

'What did it feel like?' Steve asked.

'THAT WAS INCREDIBLE!' Keiron gasped, his eyes blazing, still trying to catch his breath and laugh at the same time.

'You fell thirty feet you idiot – why are you laughing? You should be dead!' Steve shouted, half smiling and half mystified.

'I jumped to the Moon and back, man. Why wouldn't I be laughing?' Keiron joked. Joseph and the others couldn't help but giggle along with him too.

'You see what I mean? By the way, Keiron, the armoured suit broke your fall – it protected you,' Zaan interrupted. 'See, there's no way you could possibly be human and jump that high!'

'The disc?' Steve said.

'The disc will only enhance what you've got already,' Zaan replied. 'If you were human you wouldn't have jumped a quarter as high – disc or no disc.'

'You said we're on another planet, right?' Steve puzzled, still trying to figure things out in his head. 'Then if we are, this place should have zero gravity. It wouldn't be a problem to jump that high.' The others looked on and agreed.

'He's right,' Sarah said, thinking of her science lessons.

'Think about it?' Zaan continued, 'If this were a zero gravity planet, then walking would be bouncy and cumbersome? Wouldn't it? You'd be floating everywhere. Yet you can all walk perfectly well,' he said with confidence. 'Ether World is the same as Earth in that respect. You can also breathe too.'

'So, we're all Ether-uns?' Jenna tried to say, not sounding convinced.

'Etherians, yes,' Zaan corrected, thinking, boy, these kids are stupid.

'So, all five of our lives have been a lie?' Jenna continued with tears in her eyes.

''Fraid so,' Zaan replied with little or no feeling at all.

'Where does that leave us? What was the purpose of this whole thing?' Joseph questioned, handing back the spectacles to Keiron, after lifting him to his feet.

'As I've said, you're going to be trained up and sent back to Earth,' Zaan reiterated.

'We're going back to Earth?' Sarah sounded pleased.

'What for?' Keiron badgered.

'Keiron, why are you arguing? They're letting us go home,' Jenna retorted looking as pleased as Sarah.

'I'm with Keiron on this one, girls. They're training us up to go back to Earth? There's more to this,' Steve said sceptically. 'They're sending us back to Earth for a purpose.'

'I agree,' Joseph added. 'They brought us here in the first place. We're only teenagers, not soldiers. What is this all about, Zaan?'

'Enough talk,' Zaan grunted, 'you must win the battle first, and then I'll give you further instructions on what has to be done.'

'That's not an answer, Zaan,' Keiron pressed, but Zaan ignored him.

'Battle? What, like fighting?' Jenna said, looking really confused. 'Noooo, no way. I can't fight, I'll break a nail.'

'I, err, don't do fighting,' Sarah added. 'You'll have to find someone else. Let me go home. I have homework to finish.'

'I don't do fighting either,' Joseph added. 'I just normally get beaten up, rather than actually fight back,' he said honestly. Steve and Keiron peered at each other, at Joseph's confession.

'What, you mean you get bullied?' Keiron said with curiosity.

'Every day,' Joseph admitted. 'Yeah, the McKenzie brothers, mostly.' Even saying it brought back all the trauma of his encounters.

'How many of these brothers are there?' Steve asked.

'Oh, only two,' Joseph told him, 'they're twins.'

'Two against one? I hate that – the cowards,' Keiron snarled, a fire building inside his belly. He remembered that he was getting picked on because of his weight, at one stage, but decided to fight back. It still haunted his memories.

'Why don't you fight back?' Steve questioned, also thinking of the name-calling and gibes the other footballers in his team used to call him. He was targeted because they knew eventually, he would become a striker, and the others didn't want him on the team. He immediately shrugged it off.

'I didn't know how to do that, and with two of them – it's impossible,' Joseph responded. 'I mean look at me? They're huge, I've got no chance.'

'You poor thing,' Sarah said sweetly. She though, was secretly harbouring her own issues with bullies too, because she was smart and a spoff.

'I can't believe this stuff is still happening,' Jenna added, also hiding her own bullying secret. She, being pretty, made some of the girls in her class feel inferior. They were all battling the same things, but Joseph was the only one to really admit it. There was a pause in the conversation, and then Joseph piped up.

'Hey, where's Zaan gone?' Joseph had just realised he wasn't there anymore.

'I didn't see him go anywhere,' Jenna insisted. 'Where could he have gone?'

'What do we do now?' Keiron said, looking around the room. 'This place is just too weird.'

'Doesn't matter, we have to sort ourselves out, and quick,' Steve pressed.

'How?' Sarah retorted.

'We have to fight,' Keiron said picking up on Steve's vibe. 'You heard what Zaan said.'

'Like I've already said, I-I don't know h-how. I don't want to fight,' Sarah stammered, almost in tears.

'I-I can't fight either, it's not in my nature,' Jenna said, physically trembling. 'In my school, they teach us not to fight.'

'We all have to, we have no choice,' Steve said gravely. 'Sometimes we just have to… like now!"

'I think he's right,' Joseph spoke up. He felt all their eyes looking at him, no one really expecting him to respond to this challenge.

'B-but you said you don't fight,' Jenna said as she approached him, her face white with fear.

'As Steve has just pointed out Jenna – we have no choice,' Joseph said, shaking his head, but, in his stomach, he was battling the biggest bout of nerves.

Chapter 6

New skills

The five of them felt queasy for a moment and then it passed. They were each unsteady on their feet, and had to grab one another to keep upright.

'What's happ...?' Joseph was about to say but couldn't finish. Inside his head felt like he was floating and then it dissipated – the same feeling you get when an elevator comes to a stop. He opened his eyes but didn't recognise his surroundings. The others though, were standing right beside him, and that gave him a good feeling. He'd never felt this safe in someone else's company before.

'What just happened?' Keiron asked first, and then, 'WOW, what is this?'

'Oh my God, this place is not normal,' Jenna gasped, trying to make sense of their new surroundings.

'When did we get *here*?' Steve said shaking his head doubtfully. Sarah stayed silent and tried to take everything in.

'Nothing about this place is normal,' Joseph mumbled.

The huge space in which they were now standing resembled a vast warehouse. It was all laid out in black and white. They all stood on a platform overlooking the whole thing. It resembled a small city. There were pathways in between various sized, bland looking buildings. The blocks had windows and entrances, alleyways and corridors, but there was no actual personality to any of it.

'What is all this?' Joseph asked, confusion written over his face.

'This is the training room,' came a voice from behind. It was Zaan again. They all turned to face him. He had changed from his black and white suit into full body armour, much like theirs, only pale blue. 'You didn't honestly think I would leave you roll into battle without guidance... did you? What would be the point of that?'

'I'm sick of all this,' Keiron spat, 'I wanna go home now.'

'I agree, this is crap.' Steve stepped forward. 'I've had enough of this stupid game – I'm going home too.'

'I don't think it's going to be that easy,' Sarah said looking directly at Zaan.

'I think you're right, Sarah,' Joseph cut in. 'We're stuck here.' He looked at Steve. 'You've been outside and it's not home is it. In fact it's more like a rocky desert to nowhere – miles and miles of nothing,' Joseph said, unblinking.

'Rock Lands is a barren desert, with nothing but long open spaces.' Zaan seemed to enjoy giving them bad news. 'Here is where you must be.'

'So train us.' Jenna's soft voice surprised everyone.

'It'll take a long time to train someone, especially us,' Keiron pointed out. 'How long have we got to be ready for this battle?'

'Four hours,' Zaan grinned.

'Four...' Sarah couldn't even finish.

'You've got to be joking,' Steve said.

'What? That's not long enough,' Jenna added. Joseph looked into Zaan's eyes.

'Do you think it's possible?' Joseph issued the question.

'You have no choice,' Zaan added simply. 'You each have the discs connected to your chest plates – so we can begin.' Zaan looked energised. 'Deep down inside you are Etherians and the skills you need will come to the surface. Take time to practise, but you haven't got long,' he said.

'What do we do?' Jenna inquired, but Zaan wasn't there anymore.

'Where's he gone now?' Steve said, eyes glaring. 'He's doing my head in.'

'That man is so annoying,' Jenna spat.

'Look, whatever is happening, we have to be ready,' Joseph said. 'We all have to practise. There's open ground over there, lets go.' Everyone followed Joseph. They stood in a circle in between the buildings.

'What next?' Jenna asked.

'I guess we have to see what we can do,' Keiron surmised.

'I'll go first.' Joseph stepped into the middle and jumped up to the rafters. He knew he could do it and, once up there, he grabbed onto a metal beam. He then stood up and balanced on the cross section. Looking down he could see their small faces peering back to him.

'That was amazing, Joseph,' Jenna shouted.

Joseph leapt from the beam to one of the buildings and then to the next lower down, and finally bounced off two more until he was back down on the ground again.

'Who's next?' Joseph was looking at each one.

'I'll go,' said Steve, who loved a challenge. He didn't even think. Once he'd pushed off, he was flying up into the heavens. But he misjudged the landing and missed the crosspiece. He fell forty feet to the ground, but managed to slow his descent and gracefully touched his feet on the surface.

'What... we can fly?' Sarah's eyes were wide and if her mouth opened any wider, she'd have tripped over her own jaw.

'Yes, I believe we can,' Steve answered even more surprised.

'My turn,' Jenna said, eager to get in on the act. She leapt with vigour and had to stop herself from colliding with the ceiling. She stopped just before and didn't even land on a beam – she floated in mid-air and turned to the others. 'This is AMAZING!' she half screamed, which was overtaken with exuberant laughter. 'Come on, Sarah, you have to try this.' Sarah didn't need to be asked twice and flew up to meet her new friend. Soon all of them were floating high in the apex of the warehouse. They sat in a circle, cross-legged, still suspended.

'This is kinda cool,' Jenna squeaked.

'Yeah, cool.' Sarah looked pale, but unsteady.

'You all right, Sarah?' Joseph asked. 'You're not looking so good.'

'Yeah, err, well – not a big fan of heights,' she replied, not deviating her stare from straight ahead.

'I know what you mean. I feel a bit queasy too,' Joseph admitted.

'Rubbish, this is great.' Steve couldn't contain his excitement.

'Let's get back to the ground and give Sarah some time to adjust,' Keiron said sensibly. Everyone agreed, and they slowly began to descend.

'This is crazy,' Keiron said, staring at Steve who was opposite.

'Out of control,' he responded with a wide grin.

Just then, a disturbance in the background caught everyone's attention, and they stopped about six metres above the ground. The sound was a hiss of air and the grinding of metal.

'That doesn't sound good,' Joseph commented.

'I think it's about to begin,' Keiron assumed.

'Where's it coming from?' Sarah questioned, but she needn't have bothered – they could all see. Along the walls on both sides of the training room, little window sections appeared – too many to count. They stared with quizzical expressions. Finally the last of the doors opened and then a pause ensued.

'God, what's going to happen now?' Joseph felt compelled to whisper. Firstly, the sound of buzzing could be heard – like a small swarm of bees, deep in a cave. Each member of the team swallowed hard, eyes wide and rapidly breathing. The buzzing became louder and louder. Then... they spilled out, like honey from an upturned jar.

'What are they?' Jenna's voice was all a tremble.

The units were the size of a small vacuum cleaner. Each one was white – no one was surprised at that. They all had a propeller at the rear, which gave them motion, and a short, stubby tube at the front. And what appeared to be a camera lens mounted on top.

'They look like those screen projectors we use in school,' Sarah said.

'I doubt they're here to give us a PowerPoint presentation,' Steve half joked. Joseph then realised something that everyone else didn't know.

'Listen quickly everyone, we have powers at our fingertips,' Joseph said excitedly. 'Honestly, just try it for yourself. I know because I've already used mine in the desert.' Steve, Jenna, Keiron and Sarah looked unconvinced. 'Look if you don't use them straight off, you'll die. All you have to do is believe you can do it – your mind and the disc will do the rest. But you have to put on your visors, trust me.' Joseph looked at each of them and nodded. Without asking any questions they complied with his request.

The mini robots didn't take long to zoom in on the targets, and immediately set an attacking course!

'SPLIT UP,' Steve screamed, 'WE'RE LIKE SITTING DUCKS.' Still floating Steve and Keiron broke away from the group and headed in different directions. Jenna and Sarah's expressions were etched with fear, so Joseph engaged them.

'Can you hear me?' he said.

'Y-yes, I can,' Jenna responded over the buzzing of the units.

'Me too,' Sarah added with a nod.

'I can too.' Steve's voice flowed through their onboard speakers.

'Yeah, loud and clear.' Keiron also joined in.

'The screens on your visors will alert to attack, and will also give instructions. I repeat, you have powers, use them.

Well, good luck all,' Joseph ended. The mini droids were already firing missiles. 'Take cover,' Joseph shouted.

Jenna and Sarah took Joseph's lead and dived behind a block of buildings.

'Just watch what I do and…' Joseph didn't have time to continue, as a droid flew above. He could see its lens focusing and once it locked onto his position – fired a couple of shots. Joseph just managed to avoid them all, and regroup. He raised his hand, locked on to the object and sent a surge of power from within. The air shifted sending a force that overwhelmed the target and exploded it to pieces.

'YES!' Joseph shouted in victory, he felt so pleased. But two more were already in the same airspace. Their firepower was instantaneous and one impacted his right shoulder – sending him spiralling towards the ground. He landed on his back on a low rooftop. This felt all so familiar, and brought back the fall he'd taken in the quarry earlier. He vigorously shook his head, trying to refocus. He realised that he wasn't cut or damaged in anyway, but there was a black scorch mark on his chest plate, where the missile had impacted. He went to get up and screamed; his shoulder felt as if it had been hit with a baseball bat. This was supposed to be a training session, he thought. He tenderly got up and went in search of the others.

*

The droids had abandoned Joseph when he went down and were now refocused and pursuing Sarah. They swiftly zigged and zagged their way trying to keep up with her. But she was too quick. She dropped down into a gap between some adjacent

78

buildings, which blocked their firing line. She landed perfectly getting more used to her powers, and ran along the ground. The corridors were straight and long, and she changed direction several times at crossroads, until she lost sight of them. She eventually came to another cross section, and stopped for a moment puzzling at which way should she go? She didn't even have time to decide. The sickly buzzing of motors emerged in earshot, and she looked up to find the two droids hovering menacingly overhead. She peered at her visor; it was bleeping a possible escape route.

'You are advised to run,' a voice said in her head. She didn't need any more encouragement and surged into a sprint. There were bursts of gunfire, falling debris and smoke filling the corridor, but Sarah ran blindly through it. She could feel her heart thumping deep in her throat, as she forced air into her lungs. Run Sarah run, she willed herself on. The visor was slowly steaming up with her hot breath, and her eyes burned with the salt from her sweat. But all that running was futile... Sarah stopped!

'Oh my God – a dead end!' She was cornered, and flicked her body in a hundred and eighty degree turn, to face her enemy. The two droids were poised and about to fire. She stood, chest heaving and legs like rubber, her lip quivering. The hovering robots simultaneously exploded, debris scattering like hail. She couldn't believe what had just happened until she saw Joseph and Jenna step out into the open.

'Come on, Sarah, no time to hang about girl,' Jenna screeched, her face lifting into a steady smile.

'Wow, impressive, guys,' she squeaked excitedly and flew to where they stood.

*

Keiron was quite a way from the others and being pursued by three fast moving droid units, eagerly twisting and turning to match their victim. They were firing intermittent bursts, which erupted small explosions, some quite close to him, tearing into the surroundings. He spun around and sent blocks of highly charged air in their direction. Two smashed into one of the droids and it exploded. The others continued to attack. He managed to disable another one, with his new-found power.

It dropped out of the sky with lead-like speed, but managed to release a stray shot that hit him directly in the stomach, knocking the wind out of his lungs. He temporarily lost flight and crash-landed onto the ground. He was disorientated but sucked in air, panting heavily, sweat pouring down his face. Keiron kept his focus, and fired another shot, which connected with the final droid. He luckily knocked its missile launcher off line. But it still kept coming. He managed to grab the unit with both hands and wrestled it away from his body. To his horror a drill bit began protruding from a cavity on its underside. The high-speed drill extended until it got to the surface of the armour that protected his mid-section. The bit, rotating at hundreds of revolutions a second, touched the plate and began boring through the surface.

'Get off me, you skank,' Keiron screamed, his arms aching and sweat pooling in his eye sockets. He gritted his teeth and pushed hard against the groaning persistence of the motor. 'Help me someone,' he yelled as the tip slowly cut the beginnings of a small hole in his armour. The droid wouldn't relent and the propeller intensified.

'Get... off... me...' Keiron used all his strength, but his arms were weakening. The unit was gaining momentum – until it lightened its load and slowly eased off him. What just happened? Keiron was at a loss. The small robot lifted completely away, and smashed into the wall, like a toy plane on a suicide mission. Keiron was amazed, and soon realised why. Steve hovered over him with a smug grin of satisfaction on his face.

'Thanks Steve, how did you know?' he said with a look of puzzlement.

'Just thought I'd drop by when I heard you scream like a little girl.' He said with a large slice of sarcasm. Without responding, Keiron lifted his right hand and forced a surge of energy over Steve's head. Steve flinched and his smug expression changed to anger, until he saw the droid that was about to attack him crash to the ground.

'We all need help sometimes, Steve,' Keiron replied with a smile, his cheeks glowing red.

'I'm only here because of you, mate,' Steve retorted, 'so really speaking, I would have killed that earlier.'

Keiron just shook his head – there was no beating this guy. Keiron got to his feet and floated up to Steve's level.

'Look, Steve, there are more of those bloody things on the way,' Keiron pointed out. There was a cluster of six heading towards them.

'Maybe we can smash that lot in one go?' Steve's mind was working on a plan. 'You see that building on stilts?' He drew Keirons attention to the area. 'If I draw them under there, you know what to do?' Steve shot off and hid behind the safety of a tower. The fleet of droids were flying in sequence, searching for a target, flicking from side to side. Steve waited for them to pass and got behind them. He caught their attention and flew behind a formation of large steel crates. The attacking droids followed obediently, seeking him out. He popped up to keep their focus and they changed direction in pursuit. They began firing and it was all he could do to miss the barrage of missiles. Steve spotted the building supported by the four steel legs. He swooped down and through.

'Now, Keiron! Now!' he shouted. Keiron's timing was immaculate, and as the cluster entered the ambush section, he blasted the supporting legs with a heavy force from deep within his core. The steel struts buckled and collapsed in a split second – crushing the whole pack of mechanical menaces.

'Phew, well done, mate,' Steve said, a look of relief on his face. 'We need to get back with the others, to fight these things,' he insisted, issuing the request over the comm. 'Can you all hear me?'

'I think Steve's right, everyone,' Keiron added. 'We're better as a solid unit.'

'Is everyone still in one piece?' Joseph asked, and was answered by each of them individually. 'That's fantastic news.' He sounded really pleased.

'Let's make our way back to the platform,' Sarah screeched while still fighting a droid that just wouldn't quit. 'We had a better view of everything from there. What do you all think?'

'Sounds good to me,' Joseph responded.

'Yeah, I agree we'd work better together,' Jenna added.

Jenna was the first to arrive back and kept herself hidden. Next Joseph appeared and joined her. Steve and Keiron weren't long behind, and finally Sarah completed the crew. Joseph checked his sensors and saw there were still around ten units left. They were patrolling the warehouse, probing, searching for the teenagers.

'Let's face them head-on,' Steve announced.

'Isn't that giving them one easy target?' Keiron queried.

'I think if we all attack at once, we can overwhelm and conquer.' Steve seemed really focused.

'I think I agree,' Joseph puzzled. 'One big surge of power may do the trick.'

'I'm with you, let's smash these suckers,' Sarah said with real determination, which gave everyone more confidence.

'Wow, Sarah, where did that come from?' Jenna asked, looking completely surprised.

'I don't know.' She looked as shocked as Jenna. 'I think I've realised that the only way to get out of this is to fight back.'

All five stepped out onto the platform. They stood side-by-side, defiant and for the first time unafraid. The oncoming droids came in like a swarm of bees. But this time the teenagers were prepared. The ten floating machines were in a sequence of five below and five above – a wall of attack. The youngsters didn't move and raised their hands in front, as if telling the droids to stop. As the mini flying robots approached, the five enveloped them in an invisible net. Suddenly the machines were rendered static – the ten units couldn't move or fire. Each of the kids focused their minds and slowly imploded their power. The metal units began to crumple as if caught in an unseen vacuum. It only took a matter of seconds before the ten droids were crushed beyond recognition. The five released their grip and expelled air – the euphoria and relief visible in their faces.

'Wow,' Jenna puffed, eyes bulging. They looked at one another, and a grin of satisfaction lifted their faces.

'Well done, that was much better than expected,' Zaan gushed and appeared in front of them. 'You are prepared, so now the real battle begins,' he said, but this time there was seriousness to his voice. 'You have half an hour to recover and will then enter the arena. The ultimate fight for survival will take place there. I have the utmost confidence in you.' But before anyone could utter a word, Zaan was gone again. And, the youngsters found themselves back in the holding room. There were bottles of water and they each sat and drank. No one said anything. Deep in the pit of their stomachs was the worst fear of all. Would they survive the final battle?

Chapter 7

Gratton

Dazed and tired with their goggles strewn on the floor – no one spoke for quite some time. They sat and tried to get some stability back into their lives. They knew it would only be a matter of time before the madness would continue.

'This is weird.' Joseph finally broke the silence, swallowing the last of his drink.

'You're telling me,' Keiron added, the redness in his cheeks starting to fade.

'You know I'm still finding it hard to believe this is happening to us.' Jenna was the next to speak.

'And yet outside we have a real battle, apparently.' Sarah reminded them.

'We're different people to when we arrived,' Steve finally spoke up.

'So what are you saying?' Keiron challenged.

'I don't know Kei,' Steve replied, 'everything is so weird as Joseph just said.' Steve was sitting in the corner looking through Keiron rather than actually at him. 'We're definitely not the same kids that arrived here earlier, are we?'

'No, I guess we're not,' Keiron admitted.

'Time is ticking away. We have to prepare ourselves,' Joseph sighed, and with that, the door swished open and in walked Zaan again. There was a collective groan from all of them. Steve contemplated escaping through the doorway, but it quickly slid shut, and he closed his eyes in despair.

Zaan was dressed all in black this time, and looked like a malnourished Snape. The five of them directed their eyes on him, a tremble of fear quivering inside.

'All rested up are we?' he said smugly. There was no hint of a reaction. 'Mmmm, I detect some ill will.' But the smile stayed imprinted on his face.

'What's going to happen now?' Joseph was the first to raise the question.

There was a chorus of 'Yeah' from the others.

'As I promised this will be your final test. A battle.' He seemed really pleased with himself. 'Aren't you excited?' He was almost clapping, 'I have the utmost confidence in you.'

'No,' Joseph replied.

'What if we lose?' Sarah retorted. Zaan looked at her credulously.

'There is no losing, young lady. If you lose, you will all simply die!' he responded with a shrug of his shoulders.

'Wha... are you serious?' Jenna was gobsmacked.

'There is only winning. The enemy you now face won't take any prisoners – it's win or die.' Zaan arched his brow as if it was a simple statement.

'What enemy?' Keiron questioned, 'we haven't been here long enough to make any enemies.'

'You'll soon find out,' Zaan answered. 'It's waiting.' He looked totally excited again.

'I-I don't want to die,' Jenna sobbed, 'I'm too young to die.'

'Then don't lose,' Zaan rounded sarcastically.

'This is ridiculous – you're a tool,' Steve butted in, his anger getting the better of him.

'A tool – is that a stab at my intellect?' Zaan responded casually.

'Well if you don't know, I guess it is.' Steve narrowed a stare. Zaan glared back.

'Yeah, you can't treat us like this,' Keiron said, feeling just as aggrieved.

'I'm not treating you like anything. It's simply the only way,' he said. The door slid open again and another man stood in the corridor outside. 'Ah, it's time,' Zaan said, the wide grin returning to his face. 'Okay, get yourselves ready and I shall return.' Zaan stepped outside and the door closed behind him. The group of youngsters grabbed their masks and slipped them on. Joseph could feel his stomach turning over, and guessed everyone was getting the same jitters.

'What happens now?' Sarah was about to continue, but didn't have a chance to finish. The whole group faded away and soon found themselves transported outside. Joseph recognised it right away, he could just make out the entrance where he'd come in. The air was still humid and the powder blue sky stretched into the mountains beyond. The roar of the crowd was heavy in the air, but they couldn't see them yet. Zaan was standing by a series of glass tubular elevators – five in all. The glass itself was sheer black. Zaan was ushering them to step inside each one.

'Come on, come on, they're waiting,' he insisted.

'Who?' Sarah asked, almost crying.

'You'll see,' he explained. Reluctantly, they walked towards the tubes. Steve looked around; there was nowhere else to go to escape. Behind were three Etherians carrying what looked like deadly weapons.

'We can't go back,' he mumbled to Keiron, through their communication devices.

'No, Zaan has covered off any escape,' he said with a heavy heart.

'Looks like we've got to do this guys,' Joseph whispered. He looked at the girls – they appeared as terrified as he felt. He nodded to each of them and they nervously acknowledged him in reply. The teenagers each approached and reluctantly separated, and stepped inside… the doors swiftly slid shut! It was daunting in here, just a black circular tube. Joseph looked up and could plainly see the blue contrast of sky against the glossy black glass. The top of the tube appeared about the size of a dinner plate from down here.

'Wooow, that's a long way up,' he said, not really meaning to broadcast his fears. The floor began to elevate and all five had to steady themselves. The sky became bigger, and soon they were at the top. The platform lifted them right outside and the enormity was mind-blowing. The tube began receding, leaving them suspended on individual floating platforms, facing the centre of the huge arena. Below, sat a vast audience that filled the stadium to capacity. The people roared their excitement. The amphitheatre itself was set in tiers from the ground right up into the heavens. The audience engulfed the whole arena, and overwhelmed the five players. The heat and sound generated was like a tidal wave.

'This has got the feel of a blockbuster movie,' Joseph thought to himself. He slipped on his goggles and scanned above and below. There must be tens of thousands of Etherians here, he surmised, and a figure suddenly appeared on his screen. One hundred and thirty thousand – the numbers flashed up, giving him a totally accurate reading.

He dropped his head and probed at ground level. The lens on his goggles zoomed in, making the whole thing appear in high density. The base was flat and round. It scared him because he knew it was going to be the battleground – like a boxing ring. There was an insignia plastered across the circular surface. It depicted a large eye, complete with lashes and a lid. Joseph looked and realised that the flags flapping around the stadium carried the same insignia. How strange.

He trained his gaze and sought out the rest of his group. There was fear etched in each of them. He looked at his feet – the floating platform he was standing on was about two metres in diameter, like a metal drain lid. It moved as he did and he had to put his arms out just to keep a steady balance.

'What's going on?' Keiron shouted from his position, but was almost drowned out by the shouting. He threw up his hands in bewilderment. Jenna was paired next to Steve, and Sarah was next to him, to Joseph's left. The girls looked as petrified as him, but he tried to keep his face from showing it.

'Can you hear me, Kei?' Joseph spoke calmly, after remembering to switch his communication back on.

'Oh yeah, but it's difficult with all this din,' Keiron said, but still gave a thumbs-up sign.

'This is wild.' Steve's voice cut through the speaker. 'Never been this high before, except on a plane.'

'What are we doing up here?' Jenna squeaked. 'I feel sick.'

'I guess we'll soon find out,' Joseph said, 'try to keep calm, Jenna.'

'I can't do this – I hate heights,' Sarah's voice was dry and weak and trembling like her body.

'Keep calm, Sarah. Remember what we did in the warehouse. We can do anything,' Joseph encouraged.

'Everyone listen,' Steve commanded, 'we all stood together earlier and that made a massive difference. We defeated those stupid robot thingies,' he said, which actually brought a smile to each of their faces. 'This is no different. Whatever we have to face this time, we know we have special powers to defeat this too,' he said, lifting everyone's spirits. 'Stick together and do what feels natural.' Joseph was amazed by the speech/pep talk, and felt compelled to start clapping, but restrained the urge. Steve stopped talking and was shocked by his own words. Still with the fuzzy warm feeling evoked by the morale boost, things soon turned to positive. But that was short lived!

There was a deep penetrating rumble that shook the ground, vibrating up through the arena. The audience quietened and the hush turned to audible gasps. All eyes were then trained on the large eye on the ground. The frictional sound of rock against rock grated the nerves, and the floor began to move! The five teenagers looked on with deadly intensity. The pattern of the eye began to break away into triangular sections – revealing a blackened hole below. The crowd were quietening, as the activity below vibrated through the tiers. The wider it opened, the more of what was concealed was about to show itself. Firstly, there were bouts of grey steam or smoke billowing through the remains of the receding floor. There were also a series of mechanical sounds – thudding and clanking in heavy footsteps. Joseph swallowed hard and tried to control his breathing. The hissing white smoke or steam continued rising from the depths. What was down there? It couldn't be an animal, it sounded too mechanical.

Initially, they couldn't make it out. But finally, now the sections of the eye had receded, it began to show itself. There was a pause at first, and everyone was still.

Three metal limbs exploded through the dimness of the pit, and landed with a clang – making everyone in the arena jump! Sarah almost fell off her perch.

'Oh my God,' Sarah exclaimed, eyes wide, licking her lips. Joseph looked at the two boys and grated his teeth with tension. The situation already looked impossible.

The three legs contorted and flexed, lifting the rest of the torso from within. Everyone waited for the body of the beast to reveal itself. The crowd obviously knew what this thing looked like, but they still appeared uncomfortable. It lifted into the arena and all eight legs suspended the mechanical spider's full body. It adjusted itself until it was raised fully on its haunches. The servos rotated inside the creature's belly, groaning away almost in a purr. It was at least three metres high and the whole domed body was a glossy black. It appeared to have only one eye or lens, which was positioned at the centre. Joseph could see it spinning around freely. He took a closer look at the limbs. They appeared to be made from some kind of metal, and he expected them to be like a mechanical digger arm, but they weren't. Instead of the usual hydraulic pistons with black pipes and a silver shaft, there was apparently nothing. Watching diggers at work on a building site near his home, used to be one of his hobbies. The giant arachnid looked, to all intents and purposes... real! It wasn't going to be easy to get within range to defeat it. Zaan's voice crackled over their speakers.

'You must kill Gratton,' he said. 'This is your mission.'

'Are you nuts?' Steve cried.

'How do we do that?' Jenna gushed. 'I-It's a monster.'

'Use all you have learned,' Zaan's voice continued. 'Tap into your inner selves.'

'Yeah, right,' Keiron commented with a groan. We're dead, he thought.

'Tap into my inner what?' Sarah said with a throat as croaky as a frog.

'How many have survived whilst fighting this thing?' Joseph asked. There was a pause.

'Eh, no one,' Zaan answered truthfully.

'What? And you expect us to defeat it?' Steve said. 'Get us out of here, Zaan,' he screamed.

'I want out too,' Sarah said, physically shaking.

'Me too,' Jenna added. But before anyone else could speak, Zaan cut them off.

'There is no out,' he said firmly. 'You have to defeat Gratton or you will die trying. Once you've done this, you will be ready for your mission.'

With that, things began to happen in the arena. Firstly, a solid force field hummed into life – separating the audience from the action, so the crowds couldn't get hurt. Secondly, the force field's invisible, smooth inner wall became a pathway for the spider to reach the teenagers!

Gratton sensed there was something solid to climb, as if it were waiting for it to happen. It gradually pulled its body up the hidden surface, surges of blue energy exploding from the tips of its feet on contact.

'Guys, we've got to move,' Keiron exclaimed, his glassy eyeballs almost popping out of his head. 'We've got to do something, and now!'

'Yeah we have to, come on,' Steve said in agreement. Joseph could see Sarah and Jenna freaking out – they were jumping up and down on the spot. Strangely, he wasn't as scared as the rest of them; he'd been more scared, when the McKenzie brothers were bullying him. So the feelings he held were more subdued. He could hear the instructions like thoughts inside his mind. Like he'd heard when he fought the sabre-tooth. He knew what he had to do.

'Aim, and take out the eye,' Joseph spoke up urgently.

'What, like we did against those robot thingies?' the rest shouted.

'Well yeah,' he responded; 'if it can't see us, then we will have the advantage.'

'Move,' Keiron screamed, spotting the arachnid's imminent attack. The spider had rapidly scaled the arena and took them all by surprise. Instantly everyone separated, tearing off in different directions. They went sailing through the air on the floating platforms, using them as hover boards.

'I'm going to fall!' Jenna screeched.

'Just keep doing what you're doing, you can fly too, you idiot,' Sarah called back.

'Wow, that thing is fast,' Joseph gasped.

'We all have to keep on moving,' Steve's voice hissed over the comm.

'We can escape up there – out through the top,' Keiron said, pointing to the open space. 'Follow me,' he shouted. They all lifted high up into the eaves of the arena, and headed out. But, when they arrived at the highest point, realised that the ceiling had another invisible force field stopping them from escaping. There was one almighty crash as they all bounced off and fell towards the ground. The throng of fans in the stadium booed, and jeered. Each of the teens managed to recover their boards and swooped to the other side and away from the spider. But the mechanised arachnid didn't appear to be pursuing them. Instead it was busy doing something else.

'What's it doing?' Sarah asked curiously.

'Is it building a web?' Jenna enquired.

'It appears to be…' Joseph stopped. 'Oh my God, that's cutting off our escape!' he said. He was right; while the kids had been busy trying to escape and bouncing off the ceiling and landing near to the bottom, the spider had woven half the dome in a mesh above them.

'What are we gonna do?' Jenna gasped.

'It's cutting off our chances of getting away?' Steve realised. 'We have to stop it before it completely traps us.'

'Yeah, we have to disable it right now,' Keiron responded.

'Yeah, use our power to blind it; then Gratton will be vulnerable to attack,' Joseph instructed. 'We have to think of ourselves as weapons, just as we did in the other test.'

'I agree,' Steve piped up.

'I think we can do this,' Joseph chipped in.

'I don't know,' Jenna said meekly.

'Jenna.' Sarah looked directly at her. 'We have to do this.'

'We all aim for the same spot on its back,' Steve said valiantly.

'Watch out for those legs too,' Keiron warned.

'We'll have to attack separately, from different angles,' Sarah said.

'Spread out,' Steve screamed. They readied themselves for action. By this time half the dome was a silver mesh, glistening and sparkling like a pretty Christmas display. Gratton was inverted and scurrying across the halfway stage of its own web trap. All five teenagers zoomed in with a blast of electrical energy from their fingertips, like a whip. The white lightning from each person crackled and landed on its target... locking on. The spider was caught in a five-way attack and wriggled and squirmed, seemingly in agony. The blinding display with its white fluorescence lit up the whole stadium. The smug smiles from the teens soon turned to frowns when they realised that the eye was still intact.

'There must be another force field emitting from Gratton itself... deflecting our power from damaging its eye,' Keiron realised.

'This is no use, we have to take out its legs or something,' Joseph screamed, released his grip and redirected his aim to tackle one of its limbs. The strand of his energy lassoed around one of its legs and squeezed. Gratton realised what was happening when it couldn't pull away. Its massive beady eye focussed on Joseph and a compartment opened below in its belly. The next second, Joseph found himself trapped on the side of the dome; secured by a net of wire mesh.

'What-the-hell,' he said with a struggle. 'It's shot me with a web, like bloody Spiderman. It's made of fine steel, I think.' Joseph wriggled and squirmed, but couldn't break loose. Everything that happened next was a blur. Joseph managed to turn his head, and could see that Keiron, Steve and Jenna were all trapped in exactly the same way, all except Sarah. She'd managed to escape somehow.

'Sarah, you have to help us or that thing will tear us apart,' Joseph shouted. The 'thing' was already making its way towards them. It had abandoned its activities with the web, and was trundling along at speed.

'Do something, Sarah,' Jenna cried. She was the first in line.

'Sarah!' Keiron bellowed.

'Someone wake her up, for God's sake.' Steve's terrified voice could only be heard in the chorus of cries. The audience were on tenterhooks.

Sarah was, to say the least, petrified. Her mind was working overtime, but her body wasn't responding to it. She could hear the sounds of her stricken friends, but they were just a clouded echo in the back of her mind. She swallowed hard, the gasps of the crowd adding extra weight. Gratton was almost on them, and Sarah could see it all happening. She stood on her hover board, physically shaking, unable to move.

All went quiet then... S-A-R-A-H! It was Jenna screaming into her comm, at the top of her voice.

Sarah was shaken from her dream-like state with a start, and this seemed to kick her into action. She didn't feel part of her own body and without even thinking shot a lightning bolt from the tip of her fingers. The laser cut directly through the

96

joint of one of its front legs and severed it. The spider listed to one side and almost toppled over – black fluid pumping out of the side of its torso. Sarah thought she heard it wince. Another blast an instant later, took out another leg on its right flank, making the spider hobble awkwardly. It corrected its stance and focussed all its attention on her. Gratton was already lowering its undercarriage.

'Sarah, get out of there,' Joseph called out, already anticipating the spider's intention. He knew if she got trapped, that would be it.

She darted to her left just as a missile was launched. It marginally missed her and splattered into the wall, exploding out into a mesh web. The machine scuttled its way towards her, compensating for the two missing limbs, but that didn't seem to slow it down much. Sarah lifted high into the sky, but, when she took a quick look to see where the advancing spider was, smashed straight into the half-assembled spider's web. There must have been some kind of adhesive on the mesh because she stuck fast. There was a total feeling of deflation in the hearts of her friends. She fired off one laser shot from her right hand, before Gratton loomed over her.

She twisted her head and could see the arachnid's mandibles producing a solid arc of electrical charge which surged from side to side. The giant lens on top of its body fixed in a stare. She screamed, tears flooding from her glistening eyes. The next moment was surreal. Gratton, almost in slow motion, began to dismantle. There were huge lashes of lightning that appeared from nowhere. Lasers suddenly cut the mechanical spider to pieces. Sarah craned her neck to see all four of her friends attacking the beast. It didn't stand a chance;

it was like carving up a Sunday roast. Gratton didn't have any time to react in retaliation. It fell away from its grip on the wall, and crumpled when it smashed into the ground – a smoking heap. There was a hushed silence... then the crowd erupted into a chorus of cheers. As soon as the giant eye flickered and died, Sarah's body was released from the web.

'It must have been a magnetic charge holding you, Sarah,' Joseph said with a smile. 'And thanks, by the way. If it hadn't been for you releasing me with that last shot, things might have been totally different.'

There were hugs from the rest too. Just as before, they could feel their bodies begin to fade.

Chapter 8

The Elders

The arena was suddenly gone and the team were transported to another room. They were also out of their armour and back in their original normal attire. Ironically they each felt weird being in their civilian school uniforms again. Now, the different colours instantly depicted them – it was more comfortable in the neutral white of their armour. Each one didn't feel so grown up as they did.

'God, this place is so random,' Jenna said looking disappointedly at her school clothes. 'I like this place though,' she continued looking at the new surroundings.

'Yeah, me too, it's got… colour, at least,' Sarah agreed. The boys didn't care either way, except Joseph, but he didn't let on.

'Must be a girl thing,' Steve chipped in.

The five teenagers stood and took in the decor. It was a pleasing lime green – not the blinding white of the other rooms. The area held soft furnishings, including cushioned sofas, instead of the clinical and harsh benches of the first room. The flooring was soft too with some kind of fibre, like a carpet, but different to anything they'd seen before. In the background an array of yellow glow lamps were positioned in various places

– which complimented the rest of the room. There were weird paintings on the walls, which didn't make much sense, but no one had the energy to discuss. There was also a juice bar and a food-dispensing machine; this place had everything. At the back, and down a couple of steps was a small section housing a dining area – with a couple of tables placed at the centre. The group were all exhausted from the battle and the first thing they did was slump into the cosy furniture. No one spoke at first, each trying to catch his or her breath and calm down.

'It's nice to relax without that hard body armour. Still, I hate my school uniform,' Sarah said as she snuggled into the sumptuous material. She felt like sleeping and gave out a long-winded yawn. 'I'm tired.'

'Well, that wasn't obvious,' Keiron said sarcastically.

'Boy, I'm tired too,' Jenna added, letting the soft cushions do their work.

'Is it me or does this room have the feel of a Common Room?' Joseph asked. 'But,' he added, 'better than any Common Room that I'm used to.'

'I guess it does, especially as we're in our school gear,' Steve said slumping onto one of the ample sofas.

'Yeah, one minute we're in a battle zone and the next kicking back in this place, crazy.' Joseph was mystified by the sudden change in atmosphere, he breathed out a heavy sigh.

'Talking of crazy. That Gratton was scary, thought it had us at one point,' Keiron interrupted, bringing back the memory of what had just happened. 'I don't want to go through that again – that was way too close,' he said placing his left elbow on the arm and resting his head in his palm.

'I didn't think we were going to make it either,' Jenna admitted, absentmindedly staring at Sarah.

'What are you trying to say, Jen?' Sarah lashed back, taking offence at her accusing glare. 'Because I froze, is that it?' she said, her eyes burning and a deep crease appearing in her forehead.

'No-no... I didn't say that, did I? It's not what I meant,' Jenna countered, feeling uncomfortable. 'It was just an observation. We're safe, that's the main thing.'

'But I think it's just what you meant, isn't it?' Sarah squinted directly at her, grinding her teeth, her temper building. 'Any of you in the same frame of mind?' she said, quickly scanning each of the others.

'I was thinking the same thing if I'm honest,' Steve cut in. Joseph winced, expecting the onset of a mini tornado brewing between them.

'Well, I wasn't thinking that at all, Steve.' Jenna scowled at him across from her sofa. 'I-I just meant...' she stuttered, feeling flustered.

'I know what you meant.' Sarah was getting upset, but trying her best not to show it, the tears building behind her eyes.

'It was scary for a while, but if it wasn't for *you* releasing me from that mesh, Sarah, then it would have been the end for all of us. And a totally different story,' Joseph said trying to diffuse the situation. 'You saved us all.'

'You snapped out of it, that's the main thing,' Keiron said, also sympathising. 'We all freeze at some point... I know I have in the past. We're here and everything is fine now.'

'Yeah, you were in a tough situation,' Jenna added, trying to win her over. 'I would have probably have done the same thing.'

'But you didn't, did you?' Sarah added and paused to take a breath. 'Okay,' she said, 'I get what you're all trying to do, thanks guys,' she sighed, softening a little, and things began to calm.

'Let's hope it doesn't happen again. I hope you can handle it better if it does,' Steve announced.

'Wow, subtle, Steve,' Joseph, said shaking his head. 'You should run for office at the UN – we'd be at war in no time.'

'What?' Steve frowned and lifted his shoulder innocently. 'It's only an observation.'

Joseph had only just realised; in the past, he wouldn't have spoken out with his own opinion, not with a bunch of strangers. He would've been far too shy. But things had changed dramatically in the last few hours, and he felt like a different person now – more confident and stronger. For once he felt good about himself.

'Anyone want a drink?' Joseph completely changed the direction of the conversation, knowing the damage was already done. He got up anyway before they answered – grunting and wincing as his back and legs ached – the strain of battle taking their toll on his muscles. 'You gotta check this out, it's so cool,' he said with a brighter refrain observing the different flavoured fruit at the juice bar. He fingered his way along the line of coloured containers: Masifo, Drigswoon, Pelter, Qaula and Keess. Each title came with a different colour and different flavour, he assumed. Joseph plumped for Drigswoon. He didn't really know why, probably because he loved freshly squeezed orange juice. It was a pale yellowy-orange concoction and he wondered how it would taste. He pressed the button and there was a whirring sound and then a jar like container popped out on a tray. He picked it up and tentatively took a swig. Everyone else looked on in anticipation, glad someone else was the guinea pig.

'Mmmmm, that's nice,' he beamed, licking his lips, the cool taste pleasing to his tongue. Soon the rest of the team populated the bar. Joseph moved on to the food dispenser and picked out another strange title. The food that appeared on the tray didn't look as appetising as the drink, in fact his looked disgusting, but he picked it up and descended into the restaurant. The others finally joined him.

'What is this crap?' Keiron asked whilst trying to figure out the cutlery.

'I've no idea, Kei; mine tastes like a mixture of cardboard and onions,' Joseph groaned.

'This definitely isn't pie and chips,' Steve grumbled trying to cut his way into a blob of a pastry-like substance.

'Aren't you eating, girls?' Joseph said with a grin. But by the look of horror on their faces, he knew their answer without them having to speak.

'What do you reckon happens now?' Steve uttered as he placed his tray in the "Dispense Food" area.

'I guess we wait for Zaan,' Jenna retorted swilling back the dregs of some purple liquid.

'So far he's just appeared and disappeared, hasn't he?' Sarah added.

'We wait then?' Keiron looked at the others around the table, there were nods from all around. The chatter continued and no one noticed Zaan enter the room.

'You did extremely well,' he said. Everyone turned. 'Wasn't expecting the victory at all, if I'm honest, but you did it.' Zaan stood, looking down his nose.

'Thanks for the confidence,' Steve snapped.

'Yeah, same here.' Keiron gave a look of contempt.

'Well, why did you send us in there then?' Joseph argued, bitterness seeping in.

'It had to be done,' Zaan replied simply. 'If it hadn't worked, then we would have to come up with another plan. But to be honest there isn't one.' That seemed to calm them.

'So really speaking we are your only hope?' Jenna questioned.

'Well... yes, I think, is the answer to that.' Zaan lifted his head and looked vacant for a moment, or more vacant than normal, as if he was being fed information. 'The council will see you now,' he said and the door opened. The team reluctantly got to their feet, each one inviting the other to take the lead.

'Come on and stop messing about, this is important. We mustn't keep the elders waiting.' Zaan scolded, a look of contempt on his small face.

'Elders, sounds like something off a sci-fi soap.' Keiron chuckled. 'Where do these geeks get these titles from?' he said, still smirking. Zaan turned and saw no one was following.

'Well,' he snapped. No one seemed to want to go first, so Joseph finally stepped forward, taking the lead, and the others fell in behind.

Zaan turned and walked away and the teenagers followed behind silently. The group took a stroll through wide-open corridors. There was some contrast to the otherwise bland white; the walls and floor had a marble effect. Soon they finally arrived at another room in the vast complex. This one had tall white doors marking the entrance, which slid away when they approached. They were invited inside by the wave of a hand from a stern looking guard. Joseph craned his neck and looked high up into the eaves. This was yet another boring white room and he was already missing the contrast of the lounge. Why not decorate the whole place in different colours, instead of the drab and regimental white? He walked on, almost overbalancing, so he brought his eyesight to ground level again. When they strolled through the elders' throne room all that could be heard were their echoed footsteps, clip clopping on the wide tiled floor.

'Be seated.' A sharp voice boomed from the back of the auditorium. The five children squinted, it was much more difficult without the goggles. They did as they were asked, everyone too tired to object.

'This is rather grand. Like a courtroom,' Jenna commented as she, and the others, made their way to the seats provided. There were exactly five chairs set up as an audience. Once seated, they peered ahead. There was no stage, but five thrones suspended in the air. They were also in sequence: two above, two below and one in the middle. The thrones were all occupied by a group of ancient men. They looked as old as the furniture they were sitting on. In the middle and on a slightly larger throne, which was more or less surrounded by the others, was the oldest of them all.

'He's got to be top banana?' Keiron presumed whispering to Joseph. 'The main man – top dog...'

'Okay, okay, I get what you're saying, Kei,' Joseph agreed, not taking his eyes from the front. Suddenly they felt the presence of Zaan, who glared at them. They saw he was standing at the side, and they hadn't noticed him after they'd walked in. In fact, Joseph couldn't really remember where he went.

'I am Chief Elder Seek,' the old man announced. 'You have proven yourselves beyond our expectations,' the chief elder exclaimed. 'Have you any questions?'

'What happens now?' Steve spoke up.

'Ah yes, right to the point,' one of the others added with a gentle nod.

'I'm sure Zaan has filled you in, but I shall reiterate,' the chief elder explained. 'As you know by now, you were sent to Earth for a purpose. You are by birth, Etherians, just like us.' He raised his hands and looked at his colleagues. They nodded in response. 'You have to go back, each to your own Earth families and carry on as normal, until we signal you. You then have to meet at the destination programmed into your software. This place holds the "Accelerator" and the discs will fit perfectly into the machine,' he said. 'The signal is weak here, so when you get back to earth, you'll have more idea where it is. Once the discs have been set in place, Earth's defences will be down, allowing us to attack and take over. We need all the minerals the planet has to offer to keep our world sustained.'

'Can I speak?' Keiron spoke up respectfully.

'Go on,' the chief elder agreed.

'Why don't you just send down some of your men to do it?' Keiron waited for an answer.

There was a pause, which made the teens wonder. 'We can't,' the chief elder said.

'Why not?' Keiron badgered.

'Because... we don't know where it is,' Chief Elder Seek reluctantly admitted.

'You don't know where it is? But you must have planted it there originally, didn't you?' Keiron continued. Zaan growled in the pit of his throat, and gave Keiron a sharp look of distaste.

'It's okay, Zaan, he can speak freely. Yes, we did put it there but our people died doing it. That's why we had to have new-borns down there to acclimatise to the atmosphere. And... it's been so long that it's not showing on our sensor screens anymore, so it must have been moved,' the chief elder admitted. 'Your discs will find it once you are down there, and you are already acclimatised to Earth's atmosphere. It's way too dense for us right now,' he said, raising his eyebrow. 'Once the discs are in place, the accelerator is powerful enough to filter the atmosphere for us to use. Plus, disarm their defences.'

'Err, huh, excuse me,' Sarah soon interrupted.

Zaan raised his hand and was about to reprimand her when Chief Elder Seek raised his hand to stop him. 'That's all right Zaan, let her speak,' he said.

'What will happen to the population of Earth once their defences are down?' she asked.

'I'm afraid they will obviously try to resist and fail. If they do not comply, we will have to annihilate them,' Chief Elder Seek answered simply.

'Annihi…' Steve couldn't believe what he was hearing. 'Hold on, our families are down there.'

'No, no, your families are up here. You are Etherians,' Elder Seek insisted.

'Families we don't even know,' Steve snapped.

'You can't make us do this,' Keiron erupted, his face contorted in anger.

'No, you can't,' Joseph added. 'We don't know our families here and we're not going to kill the Earth's population.'

'You want us to help you kill the only families we know?' Jenna screamed, the room was sent into frenzy with everyone protesting in unison.

'Quiet… Quiet… SILENCE!' Zaan growled and all the bickering came to a stop. 'You will not speak until you are asked to speak by Chief Elder Seek,' Zaan insisted. The children stopped. The room noise was once again returned to a more tolerant level.

'We need those minerals to sustain our lives here. You will do as you are asked,' Elder Seek insisted abruptly.

'You can't make us,' Steve said, baring his teeth. 'I won't do it.'

'Oh, but I can and you will,' Elder Seek said with a smugness that meant he had the upper hand for some reason. The back wall opened up into a large screen. This had five different images showing different groups of people. The teens looked up, agony scrolled across each face. The people were chained up like prisoners, and all had a look of anguish. There were two older people and younger siblings in each picture. Families!

'What is this?' Joseph asked, but really he knew before it was explained.

'These are your *real* families,' Elder Seek informed them.

'What kind of sick people are you?' Jenna swallowed hard – tears forming on her fraught face. 'I have a family. These poor people should be left alone.'

'These *are* your families and if you don't comply, we will have to kill them,' Elder Seek said flippantly.

'We don't even know these people,' Keiron stated, 'and you're going to kill them if we don't do as you've asked?'

'Definitely, if you don't comply,' Elder Seek responded.

'You'd kill your own people if we don't do this mission for you?' Joseph was astonished.

'There is no other way,' the elder spoke freely.

'So, if we don't do this, our families here are dead. And if we do this, our families on Earth are dead?' Jenna said, rubbing the tears and snot away from her face.

'You really have no choice either way,' Elder Seek said. 'You have two hours and then you will return to Earth,' he said and with that all five elders faded away.

'Wait, hold on – I've more questions,' Joseph shrieked, but it was no use. He was only shouting at the back wall now. The floating thrones were still there but the occupiers were gone.

'He didn't give us enough time to get in with any more questions. Maybe that was the point?' Steve said, actually making a lot of sense.

'Yeah, if we ask too many questions, could he provide us with any real answers?' Jenna pouted.

Zaan cleared his throat in a way to get their attention. 'Come on,' he said. 'I'll take you lot back to the holding room. You can discuss things there.' Zaan herded them out of the grand hall.

The five teenagers were stunned and didn't know what to think. They walked back to wherever they were going now, in a kind of stupor. No one talked, everyone trying to take in this crazy mission. One minute they were ordinary teenagers on an ordinary world, and the next assassins. The five devastated teens sat quietly inside the original room where they were first put. They sat engulfed in a world of turmoil. What could they do? It seemed to be an impossible situation.

'What are we gonna do?' Keiron eventually spoke up. 'I don't like any of this.'

'I honestly don't know,' Jenna croaked after being silent for so long. 'I'm scared.'

'We've got to do *something*,' Steve rasped. 'We can't let this happen.'

'Yes, but what?' Joseph pondered, looking at the floor. 'We're damned if we do and damned if we don't.'

'There has got to be a way out of this,' Sarah said trembling and teary.

'It seems impossible but we have to comply,' Joseph responded, a knot tightening in his stomach.

'Time is running out. We have to come up with some kind of plan,' Keiron announced, to everyone else's dread. Steve was shaking his head, trying to figure a way out of their dreadful situation. Sarah tried to hold back tears, but couldn't. Jenna slipped her arm over her shoulder in comfort. There was a long pause as everyone looked at the floor. All they could do now was wait to see what Zaan would do.

Chapter 9

Earthbound

Zaan stepped into the room once again. He looked at the devastated teenagers, but there was no apathy in his mannerism.

'These are your final instructions,' he said.

'I'm not happy with this situation,' Sarah said, but was rudely halted, as Zaan raised his hand and gave a menacing stare.

'Don't interrupt me, any of you,' he said firmly.

'I think we've had about enough of this rubbish. You're not our keeper,' Steve ranted. Zaan was about to speak again when Steve put his hand up for Zaan to be quiet. Zaan looked as though he was going to explode.

'Don't you dare disrespect me!' he bellowed, nostrils flaring.

'Aw, shut up, mate. We're not supposed to speak, yet you're telling us that we're going to have to kill our families. I think it's time you listened to us for a change,' Keiron added with conviction. 'We're not doing this, it's wrong. So what do you say about that?'

'Let's all calm down for a moment. Look, your families don't have to die,' Zaan said with a little more apathy. 'If the governments on Earth agree to let us have the resources we need, then no one has to die.'

'You honestly think it's going to be that simple?' Joseph said joining in the conversation. 'You know Earth will never agree to this – why should they? It will lead to nothing but misery for my people,' Joseph added, knowing full well that the words *my people* would agitate Zaan.

'Look, I can't do anything about this. It's been ordained by Chief Elder Seek.' Zaan paused and actually looked remorseful. 'I can't stop this,' he said, 'I can only relay what I've been asked to tell you.' They went silent and let him speak. 'You will each be sent back to Earth, and left in exactly the same place as you were, before being transported here. The discs will still be attached to each of you. You will feel them, but no one else will see or be able to touch them, only you. This means that you will still have all the skills instilled inside. We will then contact you individually and from then on your mission will be the priority. Now… have you any questions?'

'So we have to find this machine and connect all our discs to it?' Steve said.

'That is correct. This action will drain the world's defences. This is for us to impose our influence on the people of Earth,' Zaan proclaimed. 'Once everything is put in place, you will all return to Ether World and live out your days serving your world.'

'B-but Earth is our world,' Jenna said trembling.

'Earth was never your world, Jenna,' Zaan retorted. 'I've told you that.' His temper was rising slowly. 'Don't you understand?' he said. 'You'll be free to live life with your real family here. It's simple, really.'

'But we don't know our so-called real family here, don't *you* understand? We've been living a life on Earth and that's all we know,' Jenna explained. 'I can't just leave one family and go and be happy with another.' She was upset and tears glistened in her green eyes.

'ENOUGH! This conversation is going nowhere,' Zaan concluded, eyes flashing. 'You've a job to do and that's all there is to it. Just get on with it. You'll each be summoned to a separate station, and that will transport you back to Earth.' Zaan said no more, and walked out of the room. In his absence there was silence and grim faces.

'They can't make us go if we stage a sit-in,' Keiron said seriously.

'How are we going to do that?' Joseph was at a loss.

'I saw this on the news,' Jenna said and, with that, sat on the floor. 'Come on,' she insisted. So the rest of them reluctantly all sat on the floor with her.

'What are you doing, Jen?' Sarah slumped down next to her and shrugged her shoulders.

'For a start we all need to sit in a circle, back-to-back,' she continued. They all did as she'd asked. 'Right, link arms and like protestors and just play dead – like a lead weight.' Everyone looked a bit vague at this instruction. She could see they weren't following. 'You know, so that it's more difficult to pick them up. But, we have powers. All we have to do is concentrate and repel them.'

'Sounds good,' Joseph said warmly.

'Yeah, I'm impressed.' Steve was nodding his approval.

'Like it, Jenna,' Keiron said with a smile.

'Got my vote too, Jen,' Sarah said. In that moment, the door swished open and two guards walked in.

'Hold tight, everyone.' Jenna sat rigid on the floor.

'You come with us.' The guard pointed to Sarah.

'I'm not going anywhere,' she said adamantly. The guards stepped forward but were propelled back, by the sheer force of the team's power. They got back to their feet, but could not get within a metre of the teenagers. Each one had their eyes closed and was in deep concentration.

'What is the meaning of this?' Zaan's voice was suddenly heard in the room. Instantly a weakness took hold of them. The guards moved in and were able to remove them easily. When they opened their eyes they could see that Zaan had his arms outstretched, and was exerting his power on them – weakening theirs.

'You worthless git,' Steve screamed, as more guards arrived and forcibly took him, and the rest of his team, out of the room. They were dragged along the corridors. They kicked and struggled, trying to slow down the process, but it was no use. They were eventually shoved into a single pod each and secured inside. From outside, their protests were reverberating along the sweeping passageways. The soldiers stood firm and grim faced. Zaan simply turned away and made his trek to the elders. Soon the sound of persecution dulled and was replaced with silence.

Chapter 10

Devastation

Joseph screamed and thumped in protest on the inside of the pod, but it was no use – no one came to release him. He sat on the moulded seat and dropped his head back – it gave a small thud against the wall. He breathed out a depressed sigh. Looking around inside the small compartment he realised that it had the feel of a photo booth, the ones you find at a shopping precinct. Again, everything was blinding white. He closed his eyes and pictured the others in their pod. What were they going to do once they were back on Earth?

There was a strange churning in his stomach, as if the pod was in motion. Joseph steadied himself by pushing against the sides, keeping his eyes closed. He soon got the feeling of being outside, and realised he was in a different place right away when he shivered. The temperature had certainly dropped. He quickly opened his eyes when the noxious smell of burning filled his nostrils. There was the pungent odour of scorched timber, and the overpowering whiff of molten metal. He could taste the polluted air deep in the back of his throat; it made him rasp and cough openly.

Where was he? Zaan had told them all that they'd be placed in exactly the same spot as they'd been before the abduction. But this couldn't be it.

It was dark, but that was because the light was blocked. He found himself under a section of tree bough. Joseph found he had to crawl out of his cubby space, and then thread his way through the branches. After an initial struggle of twisting and turning, he eventually got to the surface. He looked up – the sky was alive with a mixture of billowing smoke and a heavy concentration of rainclouds. Joseph rolled off and landed in a mud puddle – the rain was lashing down. He hated the rain; it always made him feel depressed, especially as a kid when he wasn't allowed out to play.

He took a moment to think back. It had been a perfectly sunny day the last time he was here. It was hard to take anything in. Then he came back to his senses, he remembered he had a job to do. He looked around but nothing made sense.

'This can't be right?' he felt himself mumble. 'What's happened?' Nothing in his immediate focus looked anything like Formby – his hometown. In fact, it didn't look like anything he'd ever seen before. What was he doing on a demolition site? He fell back onto his haunches; his hands squelched into the surface of the mud puddle. He tried to clear the bitterness in his throat, but it was difficult – the more he tried to clear it, the dryer it became. He instinctively reached for his right hip and found what he was looking for, the water bottle. He placed it into his left and wiped his right hand as best as he could before he flipped open the top. He swallowed hard, almost choking in the process. When he'd finished he replaced it back on his hip. Next a full-face mask lifted up and covered his entire head, eradicating the toxic fumes.

'Hold on.' He looked down at his body and found that he was wearing his full armour. 'This doesn't make any sense at all,' he mumbled. 'I was wearing my school uniform when I left.' He had to think back to remember. So many things had happened in the last… he didn't really know how long it had all taken. The abductions, the battles, his new friends, the elders, Zaan, the mission… everything! But why would they send him back in armour if they expected him to blend in? Maybe he could feel and see it while others couldn't? He was confused. He had to focus and make sense and tried to clear his mind. Was he in the right place?

Firstly, he noticed there were small fires that appeared to be burning in various places, as if an attack had taken place. In between all the fires were ruined and demolished buildings. It resembled a war zone from a video game, but this was real! The rain was adding to the confusion, bringing with it a grey haze.

He looked down at his feet and noticed the stream, which he did recognise. But the water wasn't clear and inviting like earlier. No, this had swirls of colour, from toxins that had obviously contaminated it. This brought him back to his previous memory of swilling the mud from the disc, before all this had taken place.

'Hold on… the disc,' he spoke freely. 'Zaan said we would still feel it.' He quickly looked at his left shoulder, and there it was. Did he have the same powers he'd found on Ether World? He got to his feet and pushed out his chest, he felt empowered. Could he do exactly the same things here?

Joseph concentrated his focus.

'So, if this is the stream near my housing estate, then… that demolition site is where I live!' His heart quickened, a sickening feeling soon filled his stomach – my family! But Zaan's words seemed to stab at his mind.

'Your family is on Ether World.' The words rang in his head.

'I can't just leave them,' he shouted, as if in conversation with him right there. He was angry and unsure of himself. Joseph climbed onto the banking and ran across the remains of the bridge. He had to manoeuvre obstacles as he went.

He came face-to-face with the full horror of his community. 'Oh my God.' He didn't know where to start. The confusion was too much to take in. The sensors on his lens were pinpointing the outlines of dead bodies, and the faint life signs of the living. He felt sick, and the lens sensed this and lifted as he bent over and threw up. He righted himself and let the rain fill his mouth. He spat out the disgusting taste and the lens dropped down again. The downpour lashed against the glass lens, and Joseph could soon hear the sound of distant sirens - the emergency services were on their way.

This must have only just happened, he surmised. Have we been bombed? Are we at war? There were far too many questions to answer. Then it hit him: was this caused by Ether World? But surely not; in order for Zaan to attack Earth, the discs would have to be fully in place. How was he supposed to contact him to find out what was happening? He felt so cut off. So assuming Zaan didn't do this then, what has happened here? This was definitely some kind of attack from somewhere. That threw up another realisation. Where were the others? And were they safe?

I've got to find them, he thought and checked his equipment. The full system wasn't on line. So he switched on his radar and communication link, to try and contact the others. Soon the inner screen came to life and all the information he needed flashed up before his eyes.

'There they are,' he whispered.

Chapter 11

Jenna

Firstly Jenna noticed that she was wearing her full-face mask. The readout on the screen was going crazy.

'Wha-what's going on?' She was confused and frightened.

'Structure unsafe – vacate this building immediately.' Her on board computer buzzed through her ears. Two spotlights automatically flickered on, one from each side of her headset. The powerful beams, illuminating a metre of white light – opening up a gruesome picture. She realised that she still wore armour.

'How am I wearing this?' she said, raising her arms. 'Never mind, I'll have to work that out later.' If she hadn't been wearing the equipment, then she guessed she would have choked from smoke inhalation within seconds. Now she had more immediate things to take care of.

'I've got to get out of here and real quick.' She assumed that she was once again in the clothes shop – the place she'd been before all the craziness of Ether World had happened. But, this wasn't the calm and colourful boutique she'd left behind. There was no music or bright lights, or mannequins draped in elegant clothes. No, all that remained now was a twisted mess and dense smoke.

'What happened here?' Jenna spoke in the muffled confinement of her helmet. She was instantly alerted to screams and frightened voices all around. Her sensors picked up various bodies with no life signs, according to her scanning equipment. Jenna could feel her stomach tighten and she couldn't help the warm tears that were streaming down her cheeks. She sobbed as she walked through the debris, not knowing quite what to do.

'He-lp me.' Jenna's audio honed in on a faint bleating voice. She immediately craned her neck and zoomed in. There was a young girl of about her age. Jenna wouldn't have seen her in normal circumstances, not without the body heat sensor. She rushed over and knelt down beside her. Instinctively, she scanned around to see what was trapping her. It was as if she'd always been part of a rescue team. It must be the disc, she surmised. The girl was pinned under a clothes rack that had a girder on top of that. But that wasn't her only problem! Jenna could see with the help of her systems that a jagged piece of metal had sheared away from its frame-work and pierced the femoral artery in her inner thigh. In essence – she was bleeding to death, and Jenna knew... it was hopeless! The girl reached out and Jenna sympathetically grasped her hand in comfort. Jenna was trembling, almost as much as the girl. Jenna bit her bottom lip and tried to hold back the tears, sucking in air. The girl's breathing became rapid and she squeezed Jenna's hand, but eventually her grip became weak and her eyes glazed over as her hand slipped out of Jenna's. Jenna swallowed back the tears; she cupped her hand to the glass visor in a bid to mute the sadness.

She slumped back against the wall, a tirade of tears streaming down her face. This was real – this was happening right now. She could feel the warmth freely trickle down her neck.

'Structure unsafe – vacate this building immediately,' the computer repeated, shaking her back to reality. Jenna realised that there was no more she could do here, she had to think of her own safety now. So, with a trembling hand, she reached out and touched the girl's face, raking her fingers over the girl's eyelids, closing her eyes for the last time.

She had to get out, and right now! A diagram appeared on her visor screen – a schematic of the whole building, showing the safest route out. She studied it for a moment, taking in the pathway she needed to take. If she strayed then that could mean the difference between living and dying. Jenna pushed forward and got to her feet, making sure that there was a clear space above her head. She was on the second floor, and it all came back to her. She'd been checking out a new dress, but that was not even of consequence anymore – not after seeing what she'd just witnessed. Jenna collected her thoughts and scanned all around. Her on-board spotlights cut a picture through the wafting smoke.

Then a yellow pathway appeared on screen showing her the way to go. She was also being updated of the dangers as they appeared. Jenna clambered over debris and through smoke and dust. All she could hear now was her own rapid breathing, and the yawning and creaking of metal joists, buckling under more weight than was ever intended. It was frightening, like being in a theme park ride that had suddenly turned evil. It was eerie, the sound of her own groaning and the confined vision inside the mask. Jenna walked at as fast a pace as she could manage without compromising herself. She came to a bridge that would normally have led safely from the dress displays to the underwear department. But the middle to end section was completely severed. There was a gap of about three metres where another crosspiece had fallen from the ceiling and smashed straight through the whole bridge – like a knife cutting a slice from a birthday cake.

'Damn, how am I supposed to get across that?' Jenna hissed. She could see that two thirds of the bridge was still intact. There was debris strewn over the flooring, and the jagged edges sticking out like a glacier. Jenna looked above the gap in the bridge, and saw that there was a rope loosely hanging from a girder in the ceiling. She could run and grasp the rope and swing across. But, what if the rope wasn't strong enough? There was no time to think, Jenna just went for it. She burst through and ran along the bridge. As she got to the end, she leapt up and grabbed the rope in mid-flight. She swung through the air and as the motion took her over the gap... the rope snapped! Jenna, still being propelled forward came crashing down on the other side with a crack. She landed on her back, still holding the rope, unable to speak.

'Ohhh,' she eventually groaned, with half the wind knocked out of her lungs, and a heavy aching sensation down her spine. 'God, I hope I haven't broken my back.' She winced, afraid to move in case she did damage.

'No broken bones detected, only bruising and lacerations,' her computer assured her.

'It definitely feels more than that,' she winced. Jenna reached out and gripped what was left of the handrail. Then with one big pull, and a lot of yelping and tears, she sat up. She took a moment to compose herself, but the sound of the building creaking and shuddering, made her mind up for her. Jenna got to her feet, feeling light-headed.

'Right, where do I go now?' she said, trying to focus on her next move. She realised that she'd found the fire escape. But the joy that it should have brought was muted by another problem – a girder was blocking that way too. The shop was renowned for its open rustic display of exposed metal, and the girder, once a shop trademark, was now a deadly obstacle.

'Oh for God's sake, give me a break,' she cursed. The other problem was that the beam had somehow wedged itself under the push-bar of the escape door.

'How on earth did that happen?' she said, shaking her head.

'Danger! Danger! Roof about to collapse! Danger! Danger! –Roof about to collapse!' the computer repeated. Jenna began to panic – she had to move fast. The handle was jammed solid. It was crazy really. If the girder had fallen on top of it, it would have pushed it open easily. But because it was underneath, she couldn't push the bar down! Jenna grabbed it in a weak attempt to release it, fully knowing that it was useless trying. The only way was to move it down to open the door! Suddenly, a small fire erupted and sent a flame across the room – like a flame-thrower – making Jenna scream and dive for cover. The sprinklers were activated and rain fell freely from the ceiling. It was imperative that she got out right now while this gave her a momentary break. The heavy downpour from the sprinklers quickly doused the flames enough for her to continue. Jenna curled her arms around the width of the girder and interlinked her fingers to get a strong hold. In the next few seconds she was amazed as to what she did. She closed her eyes and heaved – it was actually working. The huge steel joist began to loosen, pulling away from the door. She grappled with all her heart – growling and groaning – her face contorted in concentration. If she could have seen herself, she would have been gobsmacked. She was actually lifting the section of steel, which normally would have taken a small group of men to lift. When it was far enough away… she let go, and jumped out of the way, making sure it didn't land on her feet.

The three metre long beam came down with a huge clang, but was muffled by the rest of the chaos that was taking place. Jenna, not holding back, leaped over it, and quickly slapped down on the push-bar of the door. It simply eased open, after all the trouble it took to get to it. She didn't waste any more time and dived through from the shop. Once she was in the corridor, she slammed the door shut behind her. Then she kept on going and didn't look back. It was clear to move here. She could hear the high-pitched screech of metal – as if two dinosaurs were fighting a duel. The roof inside the shop caved in completely and the vibration rumbled through the corridor, sending her to the ground. She got back to her feet. Luckily for her, the structure of the passage stayed intact. Her path was relatively clear from debris as she made her way to the staircase.

The spotlights revealed that the spiral staircase was also free of obstacles. So, wasting no time, she urgently descended the two floors and ended up in the basement. Down here things were a lot calmer, obviously the dispatch team must have already made it out. She was thankful for that. The devastation from above, raged in the background, but hadn't reached here yet. Jenna saw the fire door, and was in the loading bay in seconds. She burst out into the daylight, and collapsed in a heap on the ground. Her mask eased away and the cool sting of raindrops washed over her flushed cheeks. It actually felt good, soothing even, a contrast of what she'd just experienced. She sat with her face tilted to the sky, eyes closed. The realisation returned and Jenna shook the previous thoughts out of her head. She opened her eyes and concentrated on her immediate situation.

She found herself kneeling on the ground and looking through the traffic of skips, lined up along one side of the delivery road. Beyond that was the opening to the street, and beyond that, didn't look good from where she was kneeling. She got to her feet and walked along the rain-drenched tarmac, emerging from behind the shops and out into the town. It was difficult to take in all the damaged buildings and rubble-strewn roads and pavements.

I've got to get to the others, and find out what's happened?

Chapter 12

The Park

Blinking open his eyes, Steve instantly realised the face visor, the same as Jenna and Joseph. It quickly dawned on him that he was in the middle of the bush where he'd been searching for his ball, before he'd been *abducted*. Like the others he instantly recognised the body armour.

'Why on earth am I still wearing this?' he grimaced, looking ominously at his armour. 'I'll stand out a mile in this thing.' He was really annoyed and hadn't even worked anything out yet. He tried to release the visor, but it was sealed for some reason, and then the warning.

'Safety protocols initiated!' his on board computer shrieked with its melodic cry.

'Safety protocols... what? Why are safety protocols initiated? What's triggered them?' He didn't understand and for the moment had more questions than answers. Steve scrambled out from under the bush and onto the football field. The devastation that greeted him was even more worrying. His sensors were going wild – pinpointing the various points of deadly interest. There was a huge crater where the football field had been. Instead brown soil replaced the beautiful lush greenery of the pitch. Smoke escaped the huge hole and billowed into the distance. But he could see that fires had broken out all over the place, sending dense smog into the sky. The thought of what could have happened to his parents filled him with dread.

'What has happened here?' he said. Where were Mum and Dad? He had to find them, to make sure they were safe. He got up and wondered if he still possessed the skills from Ether World, so he could fly to rescue them.

'STEVE!' Someone's call distracted him. It wasn't too far away, and he searched for where the sound had emanated. It was difficult with the rain lashing through the smoke and dust. His visor was completely saturated in thick droplets of water, and the lens had misted. He wiped it as best as he could and made out a figure standing on top of a pile of rubble. He assumed the mound of earth used to be the changing rooms. There were sections of timber in different shapes and sizes strewn all around. When he zoomed in, he recognised him straightaway – it was Keiron!

'K-Keiron, what the hell's happened here?' Steve shouted urgently. 'Come to think of it, how did you find me?'

'We have homing devices built in, remember?' Keiron called back. 'You have to switch on all of your on-board systems.' He shouted through cupped hands. He sounded slightly out of breath.

'Audio on,' Steve said and all of a sudden his full on board computer flared into action. 'I can't talk, I've got to get home,' Steve added, but didn't need to shout this time; he could talk and hear perfectly.

'It-it's too late,' Keiron said with a tremble in his voice. 'There's... nothing left.'

'TOO LATE! What are you talking about?' Steve angrily scrambled to the top of the debris to confront him, the urge to lash out at someone or anything, overwhelming.

'Your town, it's levelled.' Keiron said solemnly, stepping back.

'Shut up, you idiot,' Steve screeched and pushed Keiron in the chest. He fell backwards onto the ground.

'Look, Steve, I don't know all of it, but my home has been smashed too. Everywhere is the same. I'm angry as well,' he retaliated. 'It's not just about your family, you know.'

'Keiron-Steve, are you two okay?' Jenna's voice came over the comm.

'Jenna, yeah we're fine. Where are you? There's been a bomb or some kind of explosion where I live, and the same with Steve too,' Keiron answered, getting back to his feet.

'Same here,' Jenna replied.

'Yeah, it's the same where I live?' Joseph's agitated voice added to the conversation.

'Someone has targeted us,' Jenna said, sounding rattled. 'How this has happened is scary.'

'We've all got to meet ASAP,' Joseph said urgently.

'Hold on,' Steve cut in. 'Have any of you heard from Sarah?' he asked curiously.

'I haven't heard from her, but she's on my radar, and not responding,' Jenna chirped up. 'Why isn't she responding? I hope she's… all right!'

'Yeah, I can see her signature, but her comm is either down or… she's…" Joseph trailed off.

'We have to find her,' Keiron gasped. 'She's not dead.'

'We all have to meet up at her location,' Joseph continued. 'That's the only way we're going to find out if she's all right.'

'But what about our families?' Steve said, bitterness in his voice. 'We can't just... leave them.'

'Steve, we've all family, and it doesn't look good for any of us. We have to find Sarah and sort this mess out,' Joseph added. 'If we don't do the right thing, then it's not going to matter for our families or anyone on Earth.'

'We can't just leave them,' Steve repeated.

'It may already be too late,' Keiron said, his eyes glazed.

'Don't talk like that,' Jenna retorted, 'we don't know anything yet.'

'You're right, Jenna. Let's find Sarah and go from there,' Keiron said.

'Who has done all this? It's got to be Zaan?' Steve said, looking to the skies.

'Look, we haven't time to discuss this now – everyone make their way to Sarah's location, we can talk about things there,' Joseph instructed, knowing they didn't have much time.

'Who put you in charge?' Steve growled. 'You're not in charge of me.'

'Are we going to do this now, Steve?' Joseph shot back. 'We're in the middle of a warzone by the look of things, and we don't even know who or what we're up against, so why fight amongst ourselves?'

'It's got to be Zaan,' Jenna's voice cut in.

'Like Joseph said, we don't know anything for sure at the moment,' Keiron chipped in.

'Let's find Sarah and then we can work out what's happened with our families,' Joseph said sensibly. 'Is that okay with you, Steve?' There was a pause.

'Sorry, you're right, I'm just upset,' Steve admitted.

'We all are.' Keiron turned to him and squeezed his shoulder, not that he could feel it through the armour. This brought another question from Keiron.

'Why are we wearing our armour?' he said.

'That's something else we'll have to find out eventually. Have you all got Sarah's co-ordinates on screen?' Joseph asked.

They all answered, in succession.

'Hold on a minute.' Jenna sounded concerned. 'I see something. Let me take a closer look and I'll get back to you.' They waited, the rain coming down in waves from black storm clouds.

'Jenna... what is it?' Keiron felt the need to whisper. 'What do you see?'

'Wait a minute. I think there are soldiers,' she said.

'Well that would make sense bearing in mind there's been explosions,' Steve said. 'Yeah, I mean the army would have to be called in.'

'But it doesn't look like the British Army – they look strange from here... different – metallic,' Jenna explained.

'What do you mean – metallic?' Joseph asked.

'What, like robots?' Keiron said it exactly the same time as Jenna.

'Robots!' Jenna exclaimed in unison.

'Are you winding us up?' Steve snapped. 'Robots, come on. Where the hell would robots come from?'

'I don't know. I'm only telling you what I can see,' Jenna recoiled. 'They look mechanical.'

'Jenna, stay low and try to stay hidden,' Joseph said and then his comm went quiet.

'Joseph... Joseph, are you there?' Keiron blasted over the comm.

'I see them too, Jenna. She's right, they are here too, and I don't recognise the uniforms. If I didn't know any better, I would say they're robots too.'

'Are you serious?' Keiron said excitedly. 'What, like on *The Terminator*?'

'Nothing makes sense anymore,' Jenna shrieked.

'Everyone, we've got to assume this is some kind of invasion, either from Ether World or somewhere else completely. Zaan needed us to set things in motion so why would he send these things to slow the process down? I think this is out of his hands too.'

'Hold on, hold on,' Keiron shrieked excitedly, 'I see them too,' he hissed, lowering his voice. 'They're here.'

'Where? Where?' Steve asked, looking totally sceptical.

'There, look – straight ahead.' Keiron pointed in the direction of a cluster of black smoke, and movement emerging through it. Steve waited and concentrated his focus. His breathing became rapid and he licked his lips.

'Oh... hold on... yeah, I see them now,' Steve's voice calmed over the speakers. 'What are they doing here? This is weird,' he said, his eyes wide.

'Are they all dressed in the same black uniform and kind of robotic?' Jenna said sarcastically.

'All right, Jen, you were right,' Steve admitted. 'But this puts a whole new twist to our mission.'

'Yeah, this operation was supposed to be a covert mission,' Keiron said, remembering the Xbox game he'd been playing recently.

'Covert mission? Who do you think you are, Ethan Hunt?' Steve said flippantly.

'Okay, enough banter. We need to find Sarah. We need to make sure she's all right. She's also got the fifth disc.' Joseph sounded more urgent now.

'They're everywhere,' Jenna whispered. 'I've got to go before I'm spotted.'

'You go, Jenna,' Joseph said with conviction.

'This doesn't look like an attack from Ether World,' Steve said. 'They've got our so-called families up there to blackmail us. Why would they send in these to mess everything up?'

'That's true,' Keiron added. 'No, I think this is something else.'

'Okay, boys, don't get caught,' Joseph said and then his voice hushed.

The four teenagers were all a fair way from the location of Sarah's signal. Steve and Keiron travelled together, and cut across country. Joseph cut through the backstreets trying to stay hidden. He then climbed over someone's garden fence and headed towards the woods. Jenna did the same. It was the most scared she'd ever felt. This reminded her of when she was a kid playing hide-and-seek. But that was years ago and only a game. This was for real, and she was frightened. Soon all four dots were close to the destination point. For a while everyone kept quiet and the "dead air" on their communications devices was eerie. The rain continued to fall and just the sound of heavy breathing filtered through the speakers. It was hard going across country; the wet muddy fields drained the energy. None of them used their power to fly just in case they were spotted and shot down. As they got closer to Sarah's town, Joseph spoke up.

'I see a steeple, a church maybe,' Joseph cut through the dead air. 'Let's meet up there.' He heard the others agree with whispers.

'We'll see you there,' Keiron answered.

Sarah's town was in much the same state as the others. Buildings were destroyed and the same picture of peppered fires breaking out. Also the black concentration of the robot army seemed everywhere. They'd never seen anything like this before. But there again their lives had changed completely in the last few hours.

'We're pretty close, Joe. We should be there soon,' Steve whispered.

'The robots are everywhere, Joe. Keep your head down,' Keiron added.

'Will do,' Joseph answered.

There was damage to one side of the church – the roof and part of the back wall had collapsed. Smoke billowed from around the grounds, but the building itself seemed relatively intact. Joseph scrambled in from the trees and hid behind a pub. There were silver barrels stacked up outside and he took cover when he heard noises nearby. Joseph finally got to the church and Steve and Keiron were already hidden inside; Joseph could see their blips on his screen. He was glad to see them in person though.

'Are you two okay?' he said as he climbed over the back wall.

'Yeah, we're fine.' Steve gave him a gentle slap on his back.

'Jenna's not far away,' Keiron said checking out his radarscope. They waited and, sure enough, she joined them too.

'Boy, are we glad to see you,' Keiron admitted.

'Me too,' she responded and there were hugs all round. The church stood at the top of a hill, overlooking the town of Harden. And they all peered down into the remains of the once picturesque beauty spot.

'We need a plan,' Steve confessed and all agreed.

Chapter 13

Sarah

They'd all arrived in the back yard of the church. There was a large hole where the window had been blown out, and the edge of the roof had lost a fair few slates.

'Let's go inside quickly, we've less chance of being seen in there,' Keiron said, his breath misting up the glass lens of his visor.

'Good idea,' Steve agreed. Once inside, they each removed their headgear, to gasps of relief.

'I hate that thing,' Jenna complained as she pulled the band from her ponytail, threw back her head and scrunched her hair until it fell onto her shoulders. Joseph realised the difference between the two genders in just that one action. He took his off and wiped the sweat from his brow with the back of his hand, like the other two boys, not caring how they looked. Girls did things a different way. She seemed prettier, even with the flushed cheeks and a smidge of dirt on her forehead. Joseph shook from his thoughts and looked away, trying not to be too obvious.

He took a breath and checked out the inner surroundings of the church. The rain was dripping in through the newly made hole, and also tinkled against the stained glass windows that remained intact. It was so sad to see this old building in such a state, even though he'd never been there before. He could picture it in its former glory. The wall had collapsed and the bricks had smashed into the back two rows of benches – demolishing them. The font was also in pieces, like a giant 3D jigsaw with only the base remaining. He shook his head in dismay. He looked to the altar, and there was a cross to one side with Jesus impaled upon it, his sad face gazing at the damage.

'This is so messed up,' Jenna said, looking particularly tense, 'to see the place where you live, and were brought up, change so much in a such a short time.'

'Yeah, I think we all feel the same way,' Joseph nodded. 'But it's happened and there's nothing we can do about it.'

'Once this is all sorted, we've got to go and make sure our parents are all right,' Steve interjected, with a deep look of concern.

'Oh, I totally agree,' Keiron added in sympathy.

'So what do we do now?' Jenna rolled her eyes to each one, waiting for an answer.

'Well, I've still got Sarah on my radar.' Joseph peered into the mask in his hands. 'Her blip is still there even though she's not answering.'

'Well, she must definitely be here,' Keiron assumed, checking out the same blip in his visor. 'Not far away, either.'

'Her *signal* is here, right!' Joseph added with a hint of darkness. 'Doesn't mean *she's* here, though, does it?' he said with a sceptical look.

'What do you mean?' Steve probed, eyes squinting.

'Yeah, I don't understand either,' Jenna commented.

'Well, if she's here, why hasn't she contacted us?' Joseph said.

'That's true,' Keiron said, trying to figure things out. 'Maybe she's hiding and can't broadcast in case of being spotted.'

'Or...' Joseph said, and pursed his lips.

'Or, nothing, Joe,' Jenna said sharply, giving him a look of contempt. 'She's fine and just unable to respond, that's all.' Jenna replied and began making her way to the entrance of the church.

'Okay, okay,' he called after her, 'apologies.'

'Yeah, let's find her first and go from there,' Steve said sensibly. 'We'll have more of an idea by then hopefully.'

'My sensors are indicating... that building.' Jenna had opened the front door a crack and pointed down the hill towards the library, which was situated in the middle of town. Ironically the structure itself was one of only a few that weren't damaged. There were however, flames and smoke billowing from around its perimeter.

'If she is in there, then I predict she's a prisoner,' Steve said.

'How have you worked that out?' Joseph pushed him for an answer.

'Number one, she's not answering her comm. Number two, and most important of all, she's in the only building that's still standing. A makeshift prison,' he said, a smug look on his face. There was also movement, and on closer inspection revealed, the same robot-like figures they'd seen earlier.

'Those robot things are everywhere,' Keiron gasped, checking his readings.

'It feels so surreal, like a dream,' Steve said shaking his head. All four stood side by side.

'It's definitely not a dream! It all changed when we were taken, and now we have to deal with it all,' Joseph said, unblinking.

'So what's the plan?' Jenna said with a shrug of her shoulders.

'We have to find Sarah and then figure out the rest,' Steve said rubbing his forehead.

'Okay, we could wait until dark and then sneak in to get her,' Keiron uttered with authority. There was a pause.

'We've done all the training and it's now time to act. It's kind of like a video game.' Joseph looked at his colleagues with his penetrating brown eyes.

'A video game! This most definitely isn't a video game, Joe.' Steve shrugged his shoulders in scepticism. 'You can step away from a game and shut it off. There's no shutting this off.'

'We've trained for these kinds of events on Ether World, guys, we should already be prepared for this; especially with the help of the discs,' Joseph announced. There was a real up beat feeling generating from him now. 'I'm assuming that these androids have sensors to track us; Sarah may have been unlucky and got captured. We've probably got on-board dampers to stop them pin-pointing ours. Moving in to get Sarah is not going to make a difference if it's day or night, if our signals are masked.'

'Yeah, I see what you mean.' Steve agreed.

'Dampers were activated after touchdown,' DISC interrupted. 'Except for Sarah's equipment. There was a problem which cannot be rectified remotely.'

'There's your answer,' Keiron added. 'She was just unlucky.'

'What other information do you have on Sarah?' Joseph asked DISC.

'I have no more information,' the computer replied.

'What weapons do we have?' Jenna queried. 'We have nothing, no guns or anything.'

'What did we use against Gratton?' Keiron questioned. 'We didn't have guns there, either.'

'We didn't need weapons because we have them built in,' Steve said gleefully, looking at his hands.

'Okay, let's test them out here before we find Sarah,' Joseph said urgently. 'Stand back.' Joseph made his way back to the hole in the wall. There was a wheelie bin by the back door of the church. Joseph concentrated, raised his hands and sent a surge of power from his hands, directing it at the plastic container. Suddenly, the bin buckled and was catapulted against the wall. It fell to the ground, resembling a toffee sweet that had been chewed a million times. Joseph exhaled and stepped back, a look of smugness beaming on his face.

'Well, that works,' Steve laughed, stepping up behind him.

'We do still have our powers. I thought I did in the department store, but was so confused – I wasn't sure,' Jenna exclaimed.

'Right then, so how are we going to do this?' Keiron pressed, thinking of how they were going to attack the town.

'Simple, we'll make our way down there, keeping out of sight, and find a way in once we're there,' Steve said.

'That sounds simple enough.' Jenna nodded. Keiron and Joseph also gave a nod of agreement.

'We'd better put our masks back on,' Jenna said while swirling her hair back into a ponytail and pulling the facemask back into position. The boys followed suit.

Joseph's sensors suddenly tuned into an urgent radio news message as they made their way outside the church. His eyes flared.

'Hold on a moment, are you all getting this?' Joseph said and rested his hand on Jenna's shoulder.

'Getting what?' she retorted. The others turned and also stopped.

'What is it?' Keiron said, but was shushed.

'Reports are coming in that five towns in the Surrey area have been hit by a series of explosions,' the reporter announced. 'We can't confirm if these are terrorist attacks or whether it's a gas explosion of some sort. All five towns are only within ten miles of one another. Radio Pleasant will keep you updated.'

'Did you all get that?' Joseph relayed. 'Obviously these robot thingies have only just arrived – so the bombing must only have happened just before we landed.'

'So they *were* trying to kill us?' Jenna thought for a moment.

'We've got to be the ones being targeted. Don't you think it's a coincidence that our specific towns have been hit? We live five towns apart, and the five of us landed when it all happened. They were waiting for us to arrive, but weren't sure exactly where we would be – otherwise they would have picked us all off straight away,' Steve assumed.

'They must want our discs,' Joseph deduced. 'Why else would anyone want us dead? It's the only thing that makes sense to me. It must be Zaan and the elders. Perhaps they think we won't do what they want us to do?'

'No, it can't be,' Jenna cut in. 'Zaan could have easily taken our discs on Ether World,' Jenna said, looking serious. 'Why didn't he? They gave us the things in the first place. No, this must be something else.'

'I think you're right Jenna. So if it's not Zaan, then who are these beings?' Steve questioned, narrowing his eyes.

'If they didn't come from Ether World... then where do they come from?' Keiron expressed. 'Are there other occupied planets?'

'There must be,' Keiron swooned, eyes bright. He loved the idea of other planets in the solar system with creatures living on them.

'This confirms it, Sarah must be captured,' Jenna reacted.

'I think you're right, Jen,' Joseph said. 'So these things – whoever and wherever they've come from – must know about the Accelerator?'

'Come on, we could be deliberating this all day. Let's get Sarah,' Keiron said. They continued outside and stopped at the top of the hill. The emergency services had arrived. They were all there; ambulances, fire trucks and police. The four teenagers zoomed in on the action. They were expecting an explosion of laser attack from the alien invasion, Or at least some kind of retaliation.

'Hey, that's strange, nothing is happening!' Keiron peered closer.

'Why aren't the police attacking the robots? They're just walking past them as if...' Steve looked puzzled.

'They can't see them,' Jenna spoke up, realising the problem.

'That's why there wasn't mention of robots on the radio announcement,' Joseph realised. 'They're invisible! But we can see them.'

'Maybe it's because we really are...' Keiron paused, 'Etherians, like Zaan said.' No one spoke for a moment or two, not wanting to believe it. Then Steve piped up.

'They've only sent small pockets of soldiers to each town, right? Why didn't they attack in large numbers; they could've wiped us out straightaway. Whoever they are, they can't come down here themselves – the atmosphere is too threatening to them. So they've sent down a small army of machines to test it. They must have to wait until the atmosphere is dampened before they can land.'

'They need the discs in the same way that Ether World need them. They've monitored the broadcasts from Ether World,' Joseph explained.

'We've got to sneak in there and rescue Sarah, and get the disc back,' Keiron said excitedly.

'There's a lot of commotion down there, now is the time to strike,' Jenna said with confidence.

'You're right,' Joseph said.

'Let's take the back streets and see if we can find a way in from there,' Steve advised. Finally the rain began easing, and the clouds were slowly breaking up. The heat of summer was already drying the pavements. The four teenagers moved stealthily, trying not to cause any attention to themselves.

Chapter 14

Siege

It would have been awkward to try and sneak through a sleepy town in broad daylight, especially when the sun bled through the cloud and smoke – illuminating the surroundings. But, after the explosions had taken place, confusion ensued. The police were already ushering the public away to their homes. Between the sirens and mayhem of ambulances, police and the fire brigade – no one was really taking much notice of anything else.

Everything was taken up in the middle of town, and so the four-strong team progressed through the back streets undetected.

'I've never been in a real situation like this before,' Keiron admitted. 'I've only ever seen this kind of thing on the news.'

'Yeah, it's different when you're actually in the middle of things,' Steve said, sympathising.

'It's scary, I don't like it,' Jenna said. You could hear the fear in her voice.

'Never thought I'd find myself in this position either, that's for sure,' Joseph added. They all crouched low at the rear of the library, behind a wall that was half crumbled. Their heavy breathing hissed over the radio. With all the troubles taking place further down the hill, it was quieter here. They were right, the library building itself was intact, whilst, around it, all the others were damaged. It was approaching four o'clock, the rain clouds had totally dissipated, but the sun was partially muted by the smog rising from the town.

'We have to get in there?' Steve said sizing up the options they had available to them.

'How do we get in without being caught?' Jenna asked. 'Looks impossible.'

'Nothing's impossible, we can find a way in somewhere,' Joseph said with conviction.

'That fire escape looks a good way in,' Keiron pointed out as the smoke wafted from behind. 'It's an old building, and there are no cameras,' he said, searching the walls.

'Wow, you almost sounded intelligent then, Kei,' Steve quipped. Keiron looked at him with a grin, letting the sarcastic comment slide by.

'I don't see any of those robots anywhere in sight,' Jenna said, taking in all the perimeter of the grounds.

'Let's get inside and see what we're up against,' Joseph added.

'Hold on a minute.' Jenna gripped Joseph's arm. 'There's something wrong here.'

'Come on, we're wasting time,' Steve said angrily. 'We need to act now.'

'Yeah, come on, we need to move.' Keiron was getting up.

'Hold on, boys, just listen to what she has to say. We're a team, aren't we?' Joseph stated. 'What is it, Jenna?'

'I don't know, but it just doesn't feel right,' Jenna said nervously looking around. 'I can't explain.'

'We've got to have more to go on than that,' Keiron responded. 'A gut feeling?'

'Isn't this just a bit too easy?' she continued. Joseph thought for a moment.

'The longer we stay here the more chance we have of getting caught,' Joseph admitted.

'If Sarah is in there, then where are all the guards who are supposed to be guarding her?' Jenna said, her eyes wide.

'Perhaps they're inside the building, or around the front?' Steve presumed.

'I don't think so. Wouldn't you have soldiers outside, guarding the whole of the building?' she said, looking deadly serious.

'This is a trap, isn't it?' Keiron said suspiciously. 'They could be waiting behind that fire door.'

'Jenna, you're a genius,' Joseph said. 'They *want* us to rescue Sarah.'

'So that they'll have all five discs in the same place.' Steve had already worked that one out. 'Makes sense, I suppose.'

'So how do we get in without them knowing?' Joseph puzzled, his mind working overtime.

'There's got to be another way in that we can use without being caught. Check the plans for the building with your sensors,' Jenna advised.

'I'm no expert on blueprints, but I can't see another way.' Joseph scoured his screen.

'If they've got all the entrances covered, I don't see how we can get in unnoticed,' Steve said, slowly running out of options.

'There's no way in on the ground level or on top without being seen,' Jenna groaned.

'Okay. How about below ground? I played a game years ago called Tunnel's. There could be a way in from below,' Keiron announced with a grin.

'Now you're definitely sounding too intelligent today, mate. Have a lie down,' Steve said scornfully.

'Funny guy,' Keiron retorted.

'That's a brilliant idea, Keiron,' Jenna praised. Their on board computers soon revealed a schematic of the whole underground tunnel system for the town of Harden.

'There's a manhole nearby that will lead into the library,' Keiron recognised straightaway as he scanned the plans. 'We could probably get in that way,' he said, concentrating on the screen. He then stopped and looked at the others – not noticing their eyes were all trained on him. He looked shocked for a moment and then understood their surprise. 'I wanna be an architect when I leave school,' he added, embarrassed, with his cheeks glowing red. 'There's nothing wrong with that, is there?' he said, trying to convince himself more than anything. But, he was right; only a matter of metres away there was a manhole cover.

'Quickly, let's get it open,' Jenna said urgently, a new energy lifting her spirits.

'Someone is going to have to keep an eye out for those robot soldiers, though,' Steve advised. 'We don't want to be caught before we even start.' He grinned, but it was already too late.

'STAY WHERE YOU ARE.' The melodic tone surprised them at first. Steve spun around and was confronted by two of the robot soldiers.

'Busted,' he spoke quietly over the comm. It was the very first time any of them had seen the aliens close up. The two androids stood tall, well over six feet to the top of their domed heads. They were each identical, with a black outer skin and a human torso. Their hands had fingers, which were already curled around the trigger of the weapons they were carrying. They didn't have eyes or a mouth, only what appeared to be a black helmet, with a visor. Were they living organisms, such as Cyborgs or fully mechanical AIs?

'DO NOT MOVE,' they said simultaneously, as one voice.

'How we going to do this, guys?' Keiron whispered. Steve and Jenna were the first in line, but Keiron and Joseph managed to stay hidden, so they had an element of surprise.

Keiron peered at Joseph, each trying to think of a way to disarm these creatures. Keiron lowered his eyeline from Joseph to the manhole cover. He made a gesture towards Joseph, which he understood immediately.

'Frisbee?' Joseph spoke quietly.

'Yeah,' Keiron said, his voice returned almost as a gasp.

Joseph dropped to the ground as quietly as he could. Keiron was half keeping an eye on his colleague and still monitoring the soldiers. Slowly, Joseph crawled along the tarmac and got to within a metre of the manhole. Keiron could see the soldiers approaching the others.

'Come on, Joe.'

Joseph could hear the strain in Kieron's tone, and knew time was running out. Joseph forced two fingers into the centre part of the disc – where the key-tool would slot in. Normally it would take two workmen to twist-lock and lift it from its position. Joseph was on his stomach and reaching forward with one arm. Was this going to work? He questioned himself. The mechanical soldiers were still preoccupied with arresting the other two, and didn't notice what was going on.

Joseph curled his two fingers in the hole, with a tight grip and… concentrated. He closed his eyes and with his newfound strength, lifted. Nothing happened! Joseph opened his eyes again and gasped.

'What's going on?' Keiron hissed, 'they've almost got them.' Joseph looked at his hand, his fingers still in the hole. He gritted his teeth and pulled! The manhole cover lifted out, almost to his surprise; it slid from his fingers and dropped with a clang, flipping over into the hole. Keiron looked on in anguish. The two robots were puzzled. The metal disc was sticking out of the hole at an angle.

'M-O-V-E!' Keiron shouted.

Steve and Jenna realised right off what was about to happen, and hit the deck. Joseph grasped the edge and tossed the cover straight at the robots' legs, cutting them down like a chainsaw slicing through a tree. The two units crashed to the ground. Then, before they'd even worked out what had hit them, Steve leapt straight on top of one and gripped its head. With one quick action he ripped it off completely. He held it high – sparks shooting from inside the neck – the rest of its body jerking and twitching uncontrollably. Jenna was onto the other one a split-second later. She clamped her arms around the head and twisted it like a jam jar lid. It made an ear-piercing crunch before it snapped off too. Again there was a flurry of sparks and what sounded like a howl from deep within the neck. The robot flinched for a few seconds until it finally calmed. The two carcases lay lifeless and headless.

'Wow...' Keiron gushed, 'wasn't expecting that.'

'Yeah, well done, guys.' Joseph looked as amazed as Keiron. Both Jenna and Steve were on the ground holding the two heads they'd just severed. Jenna looked horrified for a moment and then threw it down in disgust, while Steve had a massive grin on his face that he never wanted to lose.

'Come on, guys, we have to move these things. We don't know if they've alerted the others,' Joseph said, looking flushed.

'Let's dump them behind this wall for now.' Steve was already pulling the bodies out of sight. Joseph followed his lead, and Keiron tossed the heads with the bodies. Jenna meanwhile had found some fallen branches from a tree nearby. She expertly covered the robots so that it was harder for them to be found.

'Next move is down there,' Steve said as he peered into the darkened hole. The stink that rose up to their masks filtered into their nostrils. Jenna winced. No one seemed to want to take the lead. Keiron noticed a ladder on one side of the hole just below the rim. He knelt down to examine it.

'Look, I'll go first and you can all follow me,' he said reluctantly.

They each descended behind him, feeling for each of the rungs. Steve was the last to go and sensibly picked up the manhole cover and replaced it. They needed to cover their tracks and not give the enemy any clues as to where they were heading. The descent took a couple of minutes and all that could be heard were panting breath and the echoed footsteps on the ladder. Keiron's foot crunched on damp gravel at the base and smartly stepped out of the way for the others.

'I can't see a thing,' he said. Then a spotlight illuminated on his visor. By the time the others were at his level, he was already planning their next move.

'The route is this way,' he said, his voice carrying through the hollow bricked expanse. It was damp and claustrophobic in there.

'Hey, what's that?' Jenna said, bewildered. 'My sensors are giving me two targets to follow. One in that direction and one in that direction.' She pointed towards the library, and also behind her.

'Got to be the Accelerator,' Joseph surmised. 'We've only got two targets to follow, so it has to be the Accelerator.'

'We have to rescue Sarah first before we go searching for that. Anyway, we need all the discs to do what we have to do.' Steve's voice sliced through the dense atmosphere of the underground tunnel.

'How come we didn't pick it up above ground?' Jenna questioned.

'The rock is too thick for the signal to penetrate, I expect,' Keiron replied.

'You're off the scale today, Mr Evans,' Jenna responded with a grin.

'I know,' he responded with a cheeky smile. 'Come on, follow me.'

Chapter 15

From below

Jenna, Joseph and Steve strolled behind Keiron, who was concentrating deeply at the details on his screen. His eyes were studiously following the layout to the underside of the library.

'How much further, Kei?' Jenna complained in a whisper that rolled along the dingy tunnel – sounding louder than she'd intended. It was damp down here, and the stench, Jenna could only describe as overwhelmingly disgusting. How had she gone from a being a fifteen-year-old innocent girl in a boutique, looking for that perfect dress, to an armour-wearing soldier, who'd been thrust into saving the world? And only in a few hours! She hated being trapped like this, but she wasn't alone. The others who were now her travelling companions, were in the same position. She was pretty sure they didn't want to be here either.

'God, I hate places like this,' she moaned, and flinched when she heard a scratching in the darkness. It was head-height too, which made it closer than ever. Without warning a rat jumped out, and caught Jenna's spotlight. The creature scurried down the wall and ran along the ground. She let out a high-pitched squeak, which felt like the piercing sound of a dentist drill. It caused everyone to stop and look directly at her. Her eyes were wide under the glass frontage of her visor.

'All right, Jenna, you okay?' Joseph surged forward, but soon jumped back and gave a screech himself when he saw the furry critter scuttle over his boot. Steve quickly followed Joseph's line of vision and shuffled urgently out of the way, to avoid the black rodent too. This whole episode made Keiron stop and turn, a look of deep disgust etched all over his face.

'What the hell is happening back there?' he hissed, trying to keep the level of his voice to a minimum. 'I'm trying to work here. Do you want to alert the enemy?' he snapped. 'They're only just above us, you know.' He looked down and saw its tail disappear into a hole. 'It's a rat, deal with it – we're in a sewer, for God's sake.' When he'd finished, he closed his eyes and took a breath.

'S-sorry,' Jenna said, trembling, the hairs on the back of her neck on end. She calmed down a little, but it still sent a shiver down her back.

'This stuff doesn't bother you, Kei?' Joseph asked curiously.

'No,' he answered, shaking his head, 'I've got a pet rat at home.' He was smirking now, which made Jenna angry.

'It's okay for you – you must love this type of adventure. I hate dark cold places. In fact, I hate this whole thing.' The others could see how much this journey was taking out of her.

'Jenna, this is tough on all of us,' Steve spoke from behind. 'We're down here trying to solve something when only a short while ago, we were just school kids.' Keiron and Joseph looked on in silent agreement. Jenna stood, the tears flowing from her eyes. 'But,' he continued, 'we're all together in this… it won't work otherwise. So, it's okay to be scared; I know I am.' Steve stood there looking totally sincere. Everyone was gobsmacked and said nothing for a moment or two. 'Did that work?' Steve said flippantly, and there was a gush of air that sounded like the release of a party balloon. 'Did I have you going there?' he said, chuckling.

'You git, Steve,' Jenna gushed, realising his sarcasm, but a smile replacing the tears all the same. She gave him a gentle thump on his right shoulder. Joseph grinned – somehow he knew Steve's sentiments were too good to be true. Keiron just shook his head. He'd been totally taken in too.

'Okay, back to business,' Keiron reasserted himself back to the task, and turned. Jenna followed, but kept her eyes more focussed, the others falling in behind. It was strange, but the tunnel seemed longer below ground than looking at the distance at ground level.

'How much further, Kei?' Jenna moaned, her feet splashing in the puddles as she continued.

'Not much longer. Oh wow, I think we got it,' Keiron gushed, sounding very excited, which rippled back to the others. He was standing looking up to the ceiling of the tunnel. His spotlight was shimmering over a square hatch embedded in the brickwork. The others soon pooled around him in a circle, everyone craning their neck.

'There's our way in,' Keiron said, pointing to it. 'They won't expect us to enter from underneath.'

'It's a long way up,' Jenna said scouring the hatch.

'How are we going to get up there?' Joseph queried.

'There's a ladder fixed to the wall, look!' Steve revealed. He was right, there was a rusty set of iron rungs fixed into the wall; just like the ladder they'd climbed down to get into the sewer.

'My sensors are not showing movement in the compartment above us,' Joseph uttered, studying a live feed he'd just tapped into.

'Let's get it open then, I don't want to spend any more time down here than I have too.' Jenna shuddered, looking down each end of the tunnel.

'Me neither,' Joseph added.

'Will that hold our weight?' Jenna said pessimistically. It did look quite fragile.

'It'll have too,' Steve concluded, 'it's the only way in.'

'Who's going up first?' Keiron asked nervously looking around them.

'I'll do it,' Steve said reluctantly. 'I don't mind, really, anything to get out of this stink hole.' They all stood back as he grappled with the iron framework. He groaned as he touched each slimy rung. He clambered up the wall in no time. They could hear the flakes of rust, peeling away and falling to the ground. Finally, he got to the top. The hatch was fixed into the curvature of the tunnel. Steve rested his feet on a rung and reached up to grab the lever on the hatch. It was difficult to try and manoeuvre the bar and balance at the same time. They could hear him groan and curse as he strained. He didn't want to put too much pressure on it, just in case it snapped completely. The handle was quite rusty and they didn't need any more problems.

'I-I... can't... sh-ift... it,' he said with a struggle. 'It's not moving.'

'Can't shift what? Is that what you said?' Keiron was squinting from below. 'What are you trying to do? We can't see from down here.'

'It's an iron lever, and it's rusted solid. Hasn't been opened for years by the look of it,' he grunted. The light from his visor danced around the hatch with every movement.

'Let me have a go?' Keiron called to him, raising his voice. 'Maybe I can move it?'

'Keep your voice down, Kei, we don't know if they're within range of us. My sensors are not picking up movement, but that doesn't mean they're not close by... or even cloaked like on *Star Trek*,' Joseph said through clenched teeth. Keiron looked a bit sheepish and put his finger absentmindedly to his lips.

'Cloaked! You really need to get out more, Joe,' Jenna said.

'I like sci-fi, there's nothing wrong with that,' he retorted.

'Shut up, you two, we've got more important things to deal with right now,' Keiron scolded. 'Steve just concentrate – you know you have the strength to do it? Use your mind and the disc will do the rest,' he reminded him.

Steve stopped and closed his eyes. Instead of trying to force things he did exactly what he'd done on Ether World – took a deep breath in, and out again. He let the warmth of the disc flood his mind. Once his breathing had steadied, he grasped the troublesome bar with a fresh grip. He paused, but now, with pure energy rather than brute strength, he eased back on the lever – the bar gave way easily. Steve pulled it as far as it would allow, and the seal eventually broke, releasing the lid! He still found it hard to believe he had these awesome powers.

'How's it going up there?' Jenna whispered as loudly as she could.

'It's open,' he called back, the excitement evident in his tone. 'I've done it.'

'Steve, switch off your light before you push it open,' Joseph advised, now standing at the bottom of the ladder. 'Just in case there is someone in there,' he said. 'We should too,' he told Jenna and Keiron. 'Don't want to be giving ourselves away at this stage.'

'Yeah,' Keiron replied and turned his off immediately. Jenna followed suit. All three stood waiting for Steve to open the lid. The silence was overwhelming. The sewer sounds continued in the background. The drip-drip-drip of water somewhere, and echoed scratching, which sent a shiver through Jenna and Joseph.

'Come on, what's the hold up?' Keiron snapped.

'Okay, okay,' Steve rounded. He then pushed open the corroded hatch. It let out a long, piercing high-pitched growl, and the whole team cringed and waited for the inevitable bang when it landed... but it didn't. It just hung at an angle, probably because the dry joints had seized.

'Shhhhhhh,' Jenna scolded, but it made no difference, it was too late to stop.

'I couldn't do it any quieter,' he said. 'Well, if someone was in here they'd have sounded the alarm by now,' Steve said in his normal voice. He climbed up into the room and switched his light back on. The others could just make out his feet disappearing into the hole and the dim illumination of the room above.

'There's no one here; come on up, guys.' He poked his head down through the hole and blinded the others on the ground. After turning their lights back on, one-by-one, they climbed into the room and joined him. The room was vast and the walls were filled with their shadows as the individual lights criss-crossed. It took them a short while to explore their new surroundings. Jenna, more than any of them, preferred the cobwebs and damp of the room to the stink and slime of below. Straightaway they could tell that this room hadn't been used much over the years. It would've been way too damp to store books down here. Their spotlights hovered over old filing cabinets, and a couple of damaged chairs stacked up to one side.

'They obviously use this as a store room,' Joseph said.

'A dumping ground, more like,' Keiron moaned.

'Christ!' Steve jumped and the others were straight on their guard.

'What have you found?' Keiron asked urgently, but Steve didn't answer for a moment. Then Joseph saw what Steve had just seen. He let out a giggle.

'A mirror?' Joseph held a wide smile now too.

'All right, don't take the mick, it's an easy mistake to make,' he grumbled.

'Boo!' Keiron joked.

'Funny guy,' Steve snapped back.

'Hey, guys! – Look, steps,' Jenna gasped, instantly taking the edge off the situation. In the corner of the abandoned room was a set of concrete stairs, leading to a door.

'Switch off your lights, guys, quickly,' Joseph signalled. No one queried his demand, and soon found out why. There was a strip of white light framing the entrance to a doorway.

'That's got to lead directly into the library, surely?' Keiron presumed without looking at his screen. Then he checked the schematic to confirm.

'I'm picking up multiple movements beyond that door… and one is Sarah's signature!' Joseph stated.

'How do we do this?' Keiron queried nervously.

'I'm only picking up two signals besides Sarah's,' Steve confirmed. 'We can take two of them, can't we?'

'Do we form a plan, or just barge in?' Jenna asked.

'I say let's just smash our way through,' Steve interjected. 'If we try to open the door slowly it may alert them anyway.' There was a pause for thought, which seemed a long time in the darkness.

'Let's do it, on count of three,' Keiron finally broke the silence.

Jenna started the count… 'One… two…'

'Hold on, hold on!' Keiron almost spat the words.

'Wait… what's the matter?' Steve anxiously cut it.

'I-I think I've made a mistake,' Keiron admitted, looking perturbed.

'What kind of mistake, Kei? This could have been a disaster,' Joseph snapped, his face serious. 'Come on, mate, what?'

'I've just noticed that that isn't the room into the library,' he said nervously.

'What do you mean?' Jenna joined in. 'Where does it lead then?'

'Well, taking another look at the blueprint, I think this door leads to a set of stairs – that leads to the room where Sarah is held captive.'

'Are you sure?' Steve was getting agitated.

'Yeah, sorry. Look, bring it up and zoom in,' he said. They all did, and could see that there was another section in between – with a set of stairs, only visible with deeper investigation.

'I've gotta say, Kei. I would definitely have missed that one,' Jenna admitted.

'Me too. Well done, buddy,' Steve agreed with Jenna, relaxing a little.

'Yeah, you're the man,' Joseph praised. 'That's why you're going to make a brilliant architect some day.'

'Why is it lit up?' Another question from Jenna. 'I mean, if it's only leading down here?'

'Obviously it must come on when the other lights are switched on in the library,' Keiron presumed.

'Well, that's a waste,' Jenna pointed out; she hated wasting energy, always shutting off lights in her house.

'I don't think we need to worry about that at the moment, Jen,' Steve said, a hint of sarcasm in his voice. Jenna looked at him with a passive glance.

'Okay, there shouldn't be anything on the other side of this door, then?' Joseph brought the attention back to their mission.

'Shouldn't be,' Keiron said sceptically, probing the plans once again, just in case. He didn't want to appear totally idiotic.

'It's obviously going to be locked,' Steve assumed.

'Only way to find out is to…' But Keiron didn't have time to say anymore; Jenna simply twisted the handle and it clicked open. A pale beam of light, from a sole bulb way up in the ceiling, reflected in their visors. Jenna gently pushed the door, teeth clenched and eyes squinted in anticipation. But, there was no squeak, or long-winded screech as expected – it opened silently. None of them expected that, especially after the debacle with the hatch.

They walked in and stared up to the top. The room was indeed a stairwell. The stairs were steep and very shallow between each step. The hallway hadn't seen attention in many years. The paintwork was brown and stained, with damp patches. There were cobwebs in the high corners where the walls met the ceiling, and it was dim, even though the light through the crack in the door suggested otherwise. Joseph decided to investigate and as silently as possible climbed up. Like a cat surveying its domain on a moonlit patrol, he scaled the stairs; trying to make his body as light as possible. Apart from the odd groan and grumble from the tired, rotten wood – he was virtually silent. When he got to the pinnacle, he gently tried the handle. But that one was most definitely locked. He sighed and made his way back down to the others, still as stealthily as possible.

'We're going to have to burst in, all guns blazing,' he said.

'We don't know how much attention that will cause. They could be alerted and ready for us before we've even had time to react,' Steve said.

'Yeah, and not only that; there's only enough room for two people abreast, at the top.' Keiron noticed. 'So we'd have to go in in pairs, and that could slow us down,' Keiron added. 'We'd be in each other's way, wouldn't we?'

'So, what *do* we do?' Jenna could see they were running out of options, and however hard she tried, couldn't think of any better way either. But it made her feel better knowing no one else could.

'Wait a minute,' Keiron pondered. They could see he was working on something.

'What, Kei? Time is running out, mate,' Joseph pushed.

'Yeah, you have to have something concrete,' Steve insisted.

'Shhhh, let him think,' Jenna said, raising her hands, palms up.

'There might be another way. Let's go back into the room and let me check something else,' he said.

They all looked sceptical, but followed anyway.

Chapter 16

Team DISC

Once back inside the dim room, they had to switch their lights back on to see through the dense darkness. The four of them grouped in a circle, each light swaying like a sword.

'Keiron! Well, is there another way? Come on, you're the Architect!' Steve said with an air of impatience.

Keiron didn't answer right away, he was already scrolling through the blueprints of the building – scouring, searching. He made a couple of grunts and an mmmm. Then his eyes seemed to light up as a spark of an idea surfaced. He broadly smiled, his red cheeks lifting his face.

'What have you got, weird guy?' Steve joked.

'There is a venting system above us, according to this map. Shhhh, listen,' he said, the excitement building. Everyone stopped talking and stood still, straining their ears. Shmm-shmm-shmm; there it was, the sound of a fan whirring away in the background somewhere in the guts of the library. 'There's normally a venting system in all buildings.' He sounded as though he knew exactly what he was talking about. 'The vents run along from room to room.'

'Why didn't we hear that before, when we were in here earlier?' Jenna sounded miffed.

'We weren't listening for it earlier, were we?' Steve said flippantly. Jenna narrowed her eyes and reluctantly nodded in agreement.

'If anyone can find it, Kei, you can,' Joseph said, giving his mate a tap on the shoulder. Everyone looked to the ceiling and followed Keiron's beam as he traced a shaky line around the room. Joseph, Jenna and Steve soon concentrated their light around Keiron's to cover more area. The ceiling was so old, some of the surface was peeling and cobwebs hovered like small curtains.

'This room is creepy,' Jenna's high pitched voice broke everyone's concentration.

'Shhh,' Keiron hissed.

'Oops, sorry,' she said, not realising how loudly she spoke.

'Well, it's not where it should be – where the blue print says it is,' Keiron observed with a grumble. There was a blank space in the wall covered over in plaster, where it was supposed to be. He puffed a sigh and continued with his inspection until he eventually found what he was looking for. 'There, look,' he said, jumping up and down. 'I've found it.'

'Okay, Kei, keep still so we can see it, mate,' Steve said stiffly.

'Don't get so excited, fella,' Joseph uttered with a grin.

'Found what? What am I looking at?' Jenna interrupted.

'There, look.' Joseph gently touched each side of her head and manoeuvred her light to the target.

'Oh, yeah; thanks, Joe,' she said, touching his arm warmly. Joseph felt awkward but happy; girls never normally acknowledged him, and as for touching, that had never happened before.

'No probs,' he simply replied, his face reddening but kept hidden by the shadows.

'They must have moved it for some reason,' Keiron cut in. 'There may have been a fire sometime ago, or something else – safety measures, possibly? Anyway, it's there.' He pointed to the square grid high up the wall feeling really proud of himself.

'You really study this stuff, don't you?' Joseph uttered sounding impressed.

'Well, you know, I just like buildings. It's probably boring to other people.' Keiron felt a little embarrassed then.

'We've all got a talent for something,' Joseph responded.

'Ah, that's high,' Jenna gasped craning her neck. 'How are we gonna get up there?'

'We can easily jump that, Jenna. Don't forget, we've got powers now,' Steve interjected. Jenna looked reluctant. 'We can all do this.' He looked determined.

'I'll get the vent open,' Joseph said sizing up the gap and the amount of spring he'd have to use in order to get to his target. He bent his knees and leaned forward – resembling the stance of a skier. He was just about to push off when Keiron quipped.

'Come on, you can do it.'

Joseph was leaning forward, almost ready to go, his mind at one with the task at hand. When Keiron spoke, he overbalanced and nearly fell over. The others tried to stifle laughs, but snorting ensued.

'Fu-nny guy,' Joseph bit back, shaking his head. 'Now shut up and let me focus,' he grunted. He got back into position again and then, with one massive push, sprang up towards the vent cover. The feeling was overwhelming; the rush of air to his face – the exhilarating realisation of flight. He couldn't breathe and certainly couldn't see, especially as all this was taking place in virtual darkness. Before he realised it, he'd ascended five metres into the air. He slammed straight into the metal casing and managed to grip what he could. It was rusted through and pulled away quite easily in his hand. Gravity instantly tugged at his body and he fell backwards towards the ground. It was all over in a matter of seconds.

'Joseph, look out!' Jenna screamed, her voice reverberating around the room. They lost sight of him and everyone quickly shone their lights on where he landed. His body was splayed out on the stone floor, the vent cover still in his grip and resting on his chest. Jenna screeched, Keiron sucked in air, and Steve stood transfixed.

'Oh my God... he's dead!' Jenna cried.

'H-he may n-not be,' Keiron stammered in shock.

'He's okay – he's fine,' Steve assured them.

'How do you know?' Jenna was filling with tears.

'Look underneath him,' Steve insisted calmly. 'There's a gap.' There was a gap of about ten centimetres between the floor and his body.

'He's hovering,' Keiron gasped, 'Oh my God, he's hovering! Clever – you idiot.' He gave out a chesty chuckle.

'It's got to be an automatic failsafe,' Jenna blurted taking her hand from her mouth and wiping her eyes. Steve and Keiron looked at her with astonishment.

'Well, I study too,' she quipped back. Joseph blinked open his eyes and flicked his head from side-to-side. He breathed out a huge lungful of air.

'You nut,' Jenna joked with relief.

'How did I...?' Joseph couldn't understand how he'd got there. As soon as he got his bearings, he dropped straight to the floor with a thunk! Steve and Keiron burst out laughing.

'Shut up you two or they'll hear us,' Jenna scolded. 'It doesn't matter how, Joe, it just automatically does, thankfully.'

'Enough of this banter. Let's find Sarah,' Steve said. He and Keiron lifted the grill off Joseph's chest and dropped it to one side. They gave him a hand to get back to his feet.

'This room must be soundproof,' Keiron said in his normal voice. 'No one has come to find us.'

'Okay, let's do this one at a time. I'll go first,' Steve insisted. He sprang up and was in the hole in the wall in seconds. Jenna was next and prepared her stance and leapt. Steve caught her at the top and pulled her in. 'Keiron,' Steve called down. He jumped next, closely followed by Joseph. Soon all four of them were crawling through the dust and dirt.

'Are we all in?' Steve whispered from further in the venting. He could barely see in the confined space.

'Yeah,' Joseph replied from the rear.

'Okay, we'd better switch off our lights,' he said calmly. 'We don't want to cause any attention or it'll be all over.'

'Good thinking,' Jenna praised. They were soon plunged into darkness. It all felt suddenly hot and claustrophobic in there. The sound of the fan pumped away further along somewhere.

'I like this even less than the sewer,' Jenna complained. 'I'm taking off my mask,' she said and gave out an enormous sigh.

'I tend to agree,' Keiron groaned back. 'I'm taking mine off too.'

'Okay, okay, we'll all take our masks off, but can you all shut up,' Steve snapped angrily from the head of the line. Joseph was already way ahead of them, and was rubbing his cheeks and chin. It was a great relief.

'You'd better not be looking at my bum, Keiron,' Jenna growled sharply.

'It's dark, Jen, and where else can I look?' Keiron spat back. 'Anyway, stop kicking up dust, will you? It's flying in my face. There's nothing to stop it now the masks are off.' He coughed and sneezed, whilst trying to shield his eyes.

'Well, put it back on then,' she retorted. Keiron just grimaced and said nothing.

'Will you two shut up or they'll definitely hear us,' Joseph hissed from the rear. He was chomping on the trail of dust kicked up by all three of them in front of him.

'Yes, will all of you shut up?' Steve whispered, shaking his head in disbelief. They shuffled along in silence for a while, except for some grunting and heavy sharp breaths. 'Shhh, I think I've found it.' Steve could see something ahead. He excitedly put on a spurt when he saw it was lighter further on. When he got there he found there was an opening in the vent, which let in daylight. He slowed down when he got closer and gingerly peeked over the edge. He could see straight down into the children's section of the library. It wasn't going to be straightforward, though. There was the disc sitting on top of a desk, and there was Sarah tied up and guarded by two soldiers. But, when he leaned forward, trying not to be seen, he saw there were also another eight all around her, making that ten in all. Steve, with a bit of a struggle, managed to turn around in the small crawl space. They could all see him plainly now with the light pouring in. He put his finger to his lips, and pointed downwards, and raised his hands, indicating the ten guards. Their faces showed the devastation they felt.

'T-e-n,' Jenna mouthed back silently, her eyes wide. Steve motioned for them to shuffle back, which was really difficult in the circumstances. They reversed still trying not to make any more noise than was necessary. Each one of them had tightness in their stomachs.

'What did you see?' Joseph whispered, 'we need every detail.'

'The room is swarming with soldiers, like I said, ten at my count,' Steve recalled. 'Sarah is tied up in the corner, and her disc is in a glass case on a desk next to her.'

'What about the guards?' Jenna probed. 'Where are they positioned?'

'She's got one each side of her, and the other eight are stationed all around the back walls of the room, a gap in between. We're going to have to surprise them big-time, and someone will have to release Sarah. Once she's free and once we've got her disc, we'll have a complete team to fight them off,' Steve conveyed.

'Sounds easy,' Keiron said.

'Good plan, Steve,' Joseph gushed, 'strategy is really becoming your thing.' Steve beamed a short smile and then returned to his serious face.

'It's definitely not going to be easy, Kei. We've got to do this fast, and we must succeed – everything depends on getting Sarah back with us so the disc is safe too,' Steve reiterated. There were nods and serious faces all around.

'One thing,' Keiron said. 'They won't be expecting us to rescue Sarah from above. We've got the advantage of surprise. They won't be slow to react though, being computerised machines.' There was a pause, each one thinking of the task ahead.

'We can do this,' Joseph responded, trying to lift everyone's spirits, 'all we have to do is float down and use our powers to disable them.' He sounded confident.

'That all sounds good,' Jenna interjected. 'After all we've been through, I think we can do this.'

'Are we all ready?' Keiron whispered. There were heavy breaths and sighs.

'We need to put our masks back on, we need to see every detail on our screens,' Joseph added.

'Let's go, then,' Steve agreed. They each shuffled their way right up to the edge of the vent, and prepared to attack!

Chapter 17

Rescue

Steve reached out for the vent cover. It had slats in it so he could press his palms in the middle and easily push it down. But before he did so, he noticed that there were hinges to one side; he knew that, if he released it, it wouldn't fall. He was about to push it open when Jenna stopped him by touching his arm.

'What's the matter, Jen?' Steve whispered, a little agitated.

'I can see screws on each side, look!' she said. Steve tilted his head and realised she was right. If he'd forced it open it would have caused more noise than anything, and would have alerted everyone down below.

'Phew, good observation, Jen,' he said, praising her.

'I can get my hand through to undo them,' she said sensibly. Steve nodded his approval and eased to one side. All eyes were now on Jenna. She pushed her fingers through the gap and found there were wing nuts rather than screw heads. A sigh of relief filled her.

'Be careful, Jen. If you drop one… they'll suss us out right away,' Joseph sent the warning.

'Oh, no pressure, then?' she responded.

'Great one, buddy, that's not going to help, is it?' Keiron joined in.

'Shut up, you two, and let her concentrate,' Steve cut in.

Jenna tried to shrug off the pressure and continued. She used her index finger and middle finger to unscrew the first one, finding it difficult without the use of her thumb. Beads of sweat dropped off her brow onto the glass lens of her mask, and ran a line down to her neck. The first one twisted easily, to her joy and soon she got into the rhythm of twirling it between her fingers, but her thumb kept fighting to help. As the nut came to the end of the thread, she slowed down and slowly twisted until the last turn. It released and fell onto her fingers, which were clamped together. She pulled it through and handed it to Steve. He gave her a reassuring smile. Now the other one, she told herself.

Jenna did the same thing on the other side to the final wing nut. That one was more difficult to crack the seal. Soon it began spinning freely in between her fingers like the other, and when it got to the last rotation – she became too excited. It fell off the thread and slipped through her moist, sweaty fingers. Jenna couldn't breathe as she and Steve watched in horror as the small metal object fell to ground. The time it took seemed twice as long as it should've... and then, to their delight, it landed silently inside the pocket of a cardigan that was draped over the back of a chair. When Jenna turned to look at Steve, his mouth was open so wide it covered the bottom part of his mask.

'You jammy git,' he said, his mouth turning to a smile.

'Skill,' Jenna said cockily, rolling her head from side-to-side, but still feeling her heart thumping inside her chest.

'What's happening?' the others called urgently, but quietly from behind, oblivious to what had just taken place.

Jenna eased back as Steve gripped the vent cover again, but this time gently pushed it open. It luckily didn't make a sound and pushed away, hanging loosely in the air with just a small fluttering of dust.

Now he could see clearly with the huge square wide open.

'Let's do this right,' Steve whispered through the comm. 'We'll each climb down slowly so we don't cause any attention.'

They poised for action, and climbed out like insects escaping a poison attack. The team, once all out, floated around the vent like skydivers. The ceilings in this library were high and so unless there was reason to look up, they'd be undetected by the robotic soldiers below.

Steve signalled with his arms for them to spread out, each focusing on the victims they'd have to take; there were four of them and ten robots to take out. This task wasn't going to be easy.

'Ready,' Joseph whispered, and there was a collective thumbs up from the others. 'Now.' The four sent energy boosts down to the victims, which immediately caused mayhem. The robots were taken completely by surprise, each were propelled across the room.

Sarah, surprised at first, then suddenly realised what was happening and looked up in wonder, her mouth gaping.

Joseph landed right next to her and immediately untied her ropes. She responded by vigorously rubbing her wrists to get feeling back into them. He was about to grab her disc when a laser was fired from one of the recovering soldiers – it hit the desk, papers flying everywhere, and sent the glass case spiralling to the floor.

'Damn,' he cursed, grinding his teeth in disapproval. Sarah eyes almost exploded from her head thinking the disc had been destroyed and her contribution would be over. But, Jenna saw what had happened and remotely ripped the weapon from the robot's hands with a flick of her wrist. Joseph with his super power lifted the android in mid-air and propelled it across the room. It spiralled like a cartwheel on bonfire night, and smashed into the wall on the other side, shattering into pieces. Steve had already taken out one machine, and was fighting hand-to-hand combat with another. Jenna flew through the air and gripped the nearest one to her, in a frenzied attack, her eyes flashing – lips peeled back behind her gums. She clamped onto its head and spun it around in a three-sixty motion – completely ripping off its head. She was getting really good at this manoeuvre. Once the robot's skid-lid departed its body, bright green and yellow sparks shot out from its neck. Its flailing arms reached out manically, and then it limply collapsed to the floor. Jenna was panting heavily.

Keiron lifted two soldiers up at the same time, with his magnetic force, and smashed them together like toys; again and again and again, until they disintegrated into small pieces. He felt the surge of power stream through his body.

A scream caught Joseph's attention, but he had his hands full battling two at the same time. One had sneaked under the radar and had Sarah around the neck, squeezing the life out of her. Steve was still busy grappling in a one-on-one wrestling frenzy. A sharp bolt of light came out of nowhere and the android's head separated from its torso; it instantly dropped its arms, releasing the grip it had on Sarah's throat. Sarah, red faced, collapsed backwards, clutching at her neck and trying to get urgently needed air back into her lungs. Joseph was in the zone and stood rigid. He held out his hands... eyes closed. The amount of force he projected was slowly crushing the two automatons against the wall. Their outer armour began to buckle and creak like a bean tin slowly imploding. Beads of sweat dripped down his face and rolled off his chin. The sheer concentration it took was immense, and used everything he had. The sound of twisting metal was ear piercing until... they were completely flattened! Joseph released his grip and dropped to his knees. The robots distorted and mangled bodies, didn't even slide to the floor. They were embedded into the mortar.

Steve was still grappling with his and pulled at the wrists. The core of the android's power was nowhere as strong as Steve's, and, with one swift action, there was a humongous crunch as he tore the limbs completely from the shoulder joints. The robot itself was still moving along on its legs... tilting from side-to-side. So Steve, still holding the arms, beat it back, smashing its head until it was unrecognisable... it stopped moving as the lights in its skull dimmed! Two blasts from a weapon had them all diving for cover. Nine soldiers had been taken care of, but one remained and was firing at will.

'We have to take him out now – there will be others coming soon,' Joseph screamed out from behind a bookcase. Sarah crawled across the floor and hid under a desk. The others had taken cover in various places in the vast room.

'I'm pinned down here,' Keiron said over his comm, 'can't move either way.'

'Me too.' Steve's voice came over the speaker. 'Can anyone disarm this thing?'

'It's positioned itself by the door, blocking our escape route.' Jenna sounded muffled. 'I can't move without being hit,' she said. Joseph tried to get up, but was soon fired upon, sending him back behind the bookcase again.

'If we all attack at the same time, maybe we can overpower it together?' Steve said trying to perfect some kind of plan.

'After three.' Joseph started the countdown, 'one… two… three.' But as soon as they revealed themselves, the robot sent a barrage of gunfire.

'It's no use.' Keiron sounded disgruntled.

When all seemed hopeless, there was a huge flash of light and the frazzled body of the attacking robot collapsed. Everyone was mystified, and when they got to their feet, saw Sarah lowering her hand to her side – her disc firmly in place.

'You go, girl,' Jenna squeaked, 'Girl Power.'

'Well done, Sarah. Girl Power, Jen? Really?' Keiron quipped.

'Yeah, good one Sarah.' Joseph congratulated her. 'Now, let's get out of here.'

'Hold on, Joe.' Keiron sounded serious. He began searching around in the gloom of the smoke-filled room.

'What's the matter?' Jenna asked, concerned.

'Where's Steve?' Keiron said. 'He has to be here somewhere?' Everyone went into panic mode… then they could suddenly hear a low groan.

'God, he must have been hit,' Joseph realised. 'Where is he?'

'I can't see him?' Sarah said urgently.

'Quickly, over here.' Jenna found him slumped in a corner. 'He's bleeding.' Jenna was almost crying.

'Oh my God, he's been hit in the side of the head,' Sarah said trembling.

'Let me have a look. I've done a first aid course.' Keiron pushed past the others and examined him. 'We have to stem the flow of blood, and bandage that cut. It doesn't look too bad – grazed more than anything,' Keiron advised, feeling please with his observation. 'Is there a first aid kit in here?'

'Why is his visor down? If he'd kept it on, this wouldn't have been such a bad hit?' Joseph stated.

'No point thinking about that now,' Keiron said, dismissing the comment. 'Sarah, bandages!' Keiron insisted.

'Yeah, there's some over here in this box,' Sarah said as she sifted through a drawer in one of the desks. Steve was coming around. He opened his eyes and could eventually see them all around him.

'You've been hit, mate,' Keiron informed him.

'My head hurts,' he winced.

'Yeah, I'll have to sort that right now, and then we have to leave while we still have time,' Keiron said. 'Sarah, pass me that pad and that bandage.' She did as she was asked and Keiron applied the pad to the cut and wrapped the bandage a few times around his skull. Sarah handed him an elasticated two-ended grip and he expertly fastened it securely.

'Wow, Kei, you've done that before?' Joseph looked really impressed, as did the others.

'Well, you know,' he grinned. 'You either got it or you ain't,' he said smugly.

'All right, enough of the chit-chat... let's get him up and get to that tunnel,' Joseph said urging them on. Steve was really wobbly at first, but they got him to his feet.

'Wow, I wish the room would stop spinning,' he said, trying to focus on one point to get himself straight.

'Come on, we'll give you a hand.' Jenna and Sarah flanked him and gripped an arm each so he wouldn't fall over.

'What a way to get attention from girls,' Keiron joked. Steve gave a wide smile.

'Right, Kei, you keep an eye behind and I'll be at the front. The girls and Steve will be safer for now in the middle.' Joseph instructed.

'We need to get back to the tunnel,' Keiron reiterated. They moved out and found the door in the other room that led down to the basement. Once they were inside Keiron sealed the door closed behind them.

They switched on their spotlights and found the hatch.

'Great.' Joseph grinned. 'Let's get down there.'

Chapter 18

Matters of the Mind

They dropped down into the tunnel, taking care with Steve as they landed. Then they made their way to the same point at which they'd entered the sewer originally, before making their route to rescuing Sarah.

'How are you feeling, Steve?' Keiron asked, the dense darkness hiding his face.

'My head aches like hell, but I don't feel so wobbly now,' he responded meekly.

'Well, that's good,' Keiron chirped up. 'We'll need a fully fit Steve to finish this task,' he said. They saw the ladder rungs embedded in the wall.

'This is definitely the place we came in,' Joseph said looking up at the drain cover. There was a small amount of light pushing through the slits in the metal. 'They must be still looking for us up there,' he said gazing.

'The signal is still here,' Jenna said as she checked her GPS, the blip still pulsing away on her screen.

'Here we go then.' Joseph was feeling really nervous, as were the others. They moved along the pathway with purpose.

'Come on, we'll have to speed up. I can hear something back there,' Steve said abruptly – knowing he'd slowed them down enough with his injury. 'They'll be with us soon enough. They must have found the hatch.'

'Okay, let's get a move on,' Keiron insisted.

'I don't want to be caught again,' Sarah mumbled, her face tight with fear.

'This way. You okay to run Steve?' Joseph asked as he took the lead.

'Yeah, I should be fine,' he answered. So, they burst into a jog, their feet slapping in the muddy underground puddles, and their lights criss-crossing on the tunnel wall. Keiron stayed at the back, and kept an eye on his friend in case his injury got worse.

'Are we all locked on to the signal?' Keiron asked, trying his best to keep up. Everyone responded with their own reply.

The shape of the underground sewage system eventually changed from an arched corridor to long circular sweeps of channel. They seemed to run for miles. The panting and slapping of feet continued until they came to a split in the sewer.

'There's a fork up ahead.' Steve noted, and, strangely, he didn't look as out of breath as the rest, considering he was carrying an injury.

'Yeah,' Joseph swallowed hard, 'got it. The target is… on the left flank,' he puffed.

'Left flank, eh?' Keiron grinned to himself. It sounded more like a battlefield assault than a tunnel chase. The deeper the track took them, the less their surroundings appeared to be maintained. The muddied ground was uneven and held potholes and pockets of puddles. Everyone tried to avoid these no knowing what lay beneath. The air became more dense, and the odour, musky. There was also a stronger presence of water, which ran rather than trickled down the walls. The temperature dropped a few degrees too.

Joseph had a strange feeling that made him stop.

'Hold up everyone,' he said.

'What's up?' Jenna asked, panting.

'A dead end, Jen,' Keiron said with a heavy breath. Jenna then realised that if they'd carried on running, they would have collided with a solid wall.

'Great, the signal is still pumping away, but behind here,' Joseph grumbled. 'How the hell are we supposed to get through there?' He stood, teeth gritted scratching his head.

'Shouldn't be a problem, little man, get out of the way,' Jenna said as if it was nothing. She stood and lifted her hands up in front of her.

'Little man…' Joseph didn't have time to react before Keiron cut in.

'Wait! Hold on there, princess!' He stepped in front of her before she'd had time to concentrate her power. She stepped back, a deep sense of hatred seething inside.

'Got a problem with me, dumpy?' she said flippantly, eyes flashing.

'You can't just blast a way through. That's what you're going to do, isn't it?' Keiron nodded.

'Ah, well yeah,' she recoiled angrily. 'Why not?' she snapped.

'Because you could have the whole tunnel collapse down on us you, stupid idiot,' he scolded. 'What a tool!' he snarled.

'Kei, calm down, mate, she didn't know,' Steve defended her sharply. 'You can't speak to her like that.' He stepped forward.

'Don't tell me to calm down, and I'm not your mate,' Keiron spat back. 'Get out of my way, stick man.'

'Stick man – who you calling stick man?' Steve squared up to Keiron, ready for a fight. 'I'd rather be a stick than a bubble.'

'Aw, why don't you all shut up? You're all a bunch of losers anyway,' Sarah whined, speaking out.

'*Losers!* We came to help you, you worthless piece of crap,' Steve cursed.

All five erupted into a tongue slanging frenzy. Keiron raised his left arm to take a swing at Steve and accidently elbowed Joseph in the face, knocking him to the floor. He landed, a bit stunned at first and then realised what Keiron had done.

'You tool, Kei,' he grunted, rubbing his sore cheek, and was about to scramble to his feet when he saw a yellow glow above their heads. He held back for a moment to take in this new phenomenon. It seemed to him, the angrier and more heated their confrontation became, the brighter the yellow blob beamed. Could it be that this thing was causing all this agro, and feeding off it? Was that possible? The controversy was almost at melting point and the light was at its brightest.

'HOLD ON! HOLD ON!' Joseph screeched, but with all the arguing going on; no one was taking any notice. 'Sod this,' he said, and suddenly sent a high-pitched whistle through his communicator, which blasted through all the earpieces of the others. They all clamped the sides of their heads. It definitely broke their concentration, and they winced under the agonising screech.

'Stop that,' they all screamed. Joseph did, and they turned to him with hatred in their eyes – then they suddenly calmed. The yellow blob diluted down to dull amber and then faded away to nothing.

'What are you playing at?' Jenna bleated.

'Yeah, what did you do that for?' Keiron was still reeling.

'I've already got a headache, I didn't need a bigger one,' Steve dropped his visor and rubbed his forehead.

'Are you crazy? You could have deafened us,' Sarah snapped. 'What was that all about, you idiot?'

'What are you doing down there, anyway?' Keiron looked puzzled. 'You fall over or something?'

'Something like that; you hit me, you fool,' Joseph said, and put out his hand for Keiron to help him up.

'I don't remember doing that,' he said. mystified. 'I'm sure I would have remembered smacking you one,' he said, grinning.

'Do any of you remember anything that happened in the last few seconds?' Joseph questioned. Everyone looked completely vacant.

'Exactly,' he said.

'We came to this dead end and…' Jenna remembered. And searched her mind for the rest of the info, but couldn't get to it.

'What are you saying, Joseph? What did happen?' Steve was intrigued.

'I think we were all under some kind of mind control,' he said.

'Mind control, are you winding me up?' Steve joked.

'Not at all. It was when we were thinking of breaking through the wall. We all became aggressive, and, as luck would have it, Keiron – through no fault of his own, by the way – elbowed me in the head. When I landed on the floor I could see something above our heads. You lot were in full on battle mode.'

'What was it?' Sarah spoke up. 'What did you see?'

'I don't really know – a kind of yellow blob glowing above our heads. But what I do know is that the louder and more aggressive everyone got, the stronger and brighter it became. You knocking me down, Kei, brought me out of it. I could see it plain then.'

'Is it still here?' Jenna quizzed, 'I can't see it.'

'No, it went when you all came back to your senses. It must have been what you said earlier Jen – a failsafe to stop us going any further,' Joseph surmised. 'Obviously someone doesn't want us tampering with the Accelerator.'

'We can't let that stop us,' Keiron said defiantly.

'Let's do this again, then, but this time, try and make the cave collapse inwardly, with as little pressure as possible,' Joseph said sensibly. 'If you feel yourselves becoming angry, ease up. We don't want another episode like that taking place.'

'We do this together this time and control our power,' Keiron proposed.

'Sounds like a good idea,' Steve added. They stood in a line and each one lifted up their hands.

'Concentrate and use as gentle a pressure as we can muster,' Keiron said. 'That should be enough to penetrate the blockage and not cause any collapse.' All eyes were closed and all minds were one, and free from distraction. Soon there was movement. There was a disturbance in the dust around the rock wall, as pieces of the cave began to fall. Bit-by-bit the formation of rock slowly fell away and the cave was eventually cleared. Once the dust had eventually settled, the group could see straight through, but only as far as their torch beams could reach.

'This thing is buried deep,' Joseph complained.

'I'm wondering what else it's going to throw at us?' Jenna was still shaken from the arguing.

'We can't stop now,' Keiron said sounding positive.

'We've come this far,' Steve added, 'and if it's sending us these tests, we must be getting close.'

'I agree,' Keiron retorted, a hint of excitement in his tone.

'That's what I'm afraid of,' Sarah said, looking terrified. 'What do we have to face? What's in there?'

'This is what we've come here for,' Joseph reminded them… as if he needed to. He stepped inside first. This next section held a really dense atmosphere, which had a more eerie feel to it. The rest of the gang pushed forward with trepidation. They'd only walked in a few metres and everyone stopped. In the thick black that enveloped them, only their shallow breathing could be heard above the trickle of water.

Each teenager used the light attached to their visor to get their bearings. Jenna let out a gasp, which cut through the darkness. Her breathing heightened.

'What is it, Jen?' Keiron asked sounding concerned.

'There, lo-ok, there's something in there,' she stammered, pointing. Keiron zoomed in and realised it was a statue!

'What is that doing here? It's only an old statue, Jen. Nothing to worry about,' Keiron chirped.

'I wouldn't be too sure of that, Kei.' Steve looked suspicious. 'Nothing we've come up against so far is a joking matter.'

'Yeah, but it's only a statue.' Sarah echoed Keiron. 'What harm can a statue do?'

'Steve's right. We can't take anything likely,' Joseph said. He had the same stern expression. Things felt more urgent now and they approached the effigy with caution. The figure looked really sinister with all five lights fixed on it. It was at least three metres high and resembled a soldier, maybe from centuries ago but lacking any distinctive markings that anyone could recognise. The head was completely encased in a helmet with only a slit for access to the eyes, which were hidden in deep shadow. Its two arms were sheathed in protective sleeves. The arms themselves were criss-crossed over its broad, metal chest plate. The waist down to the ankles were protected by armour, just like the arms and chest. All in all, the entire thing was a formidable sight.

'I've studied ancient cultures and this is a new one on me,' Sarah admitted.

'Whoa, hark at her,' Jenna joked.

'Oh, grow up, Jenna,' Sarah bit back. 'Some of us do study in school.'

'Calm down, ladies,' Joseph cut in.

'Maybe it's not of this world?' Keiron surmised, not taking any notice of the squabble.

'It's a statue, let's move on,' Jenna urged angrily, still miffed by Sarah's outburst.

'Okay, but keep your eyes peeled,' Steve said trying to get focused again. They were about to move past the sculpture when they heard the grinding of metal and soon felt vibrations in the ground. They stopped immediately and stepped back. A feeling of dread filled each of them. The thing was actually moving!

'Oh my God, that can't be good,' Jenna squealed.

The whole body of the statue began to unfurl. The quiet cavern was soon filled with high-pitched grinding that echoed through the underground. Its arms peeled away from the chest, creating a small dust cloud. The head slowly craned to life and two yellow eyes glowed from within the helmet. The team looked on in horror. The huge legs broke away from the plinth it was welded to, and stepped off onto the ground. It was alive! The sound it made as it advanced was breathtaking. Every step vibrated the ground and caused dust to rise. The joints in its stone torso creaked and squeaked, like a grinding wheel.

'What do we do?' Keiron gulped. 'It's bloody huge,' he exclaimed, eyes almost bulging out of his head.

'We have to attack now before it's composed itself,' Steve shouted. Joseph leapt forward and twisted in mid-air with an aggressive kicking motion, Bruce Lee style. The stone soldier lashed out with its right hand and brushed him away as if he were an insect. Joseph went flying across the cave and landed with a bump. Steve and Keiron tried the same manoeuvre only to be dealt with in the same way.

'It's immense,' Joseph screamed. The other two boys were still trying to recover from their fall. The girls were left, and used a force of air from their hands in a double attack, to try and slow it down. The combined pressure blasted the creature back a couple of metres. It composed itself and returned the compliment with a force of its own. The girls were lifted off their feet and cast aside. All five of the team were winded and already defeated after just one attack.

'This is impossible,' Keiron cried. 'How are we supposed to fight this monster?'

'It must have a weakness,' Steve stated. 'We have to find it, and quickly.'

'We need a plan.' Joseph winced. 'Girls, you all right?'

'Yeah, fine,' Sarah bleated. 'I'm out of ideas.'

'Me too I think,' Jenna replied, staggering to her feet. The soldier was on the move, slowly ambling its heavy frame towards the stricken teenagers. Its yellow luminous eyes were fixed in a deadly mesmerising stare.

'It's slow,' Steve said, 'which gives us time. We are definitely quicker.'

'Time for what?' Joseph asked. 'Any suggestions, anyone? We may be quicker, but that hasn't helped us so far.'

'We have to stop it from moving,' Keiron said, his mind working overtime. 'If we can disable its legs, then maybe we can stop it. Just like a rugby tackle. It can't move without its legs, can it?'

'Good idea, but how?' Jenna joined the others, eventually followed by Sarah.

'The disc – use the disc's knowledge and concentrate,' Joseph remembered.

They had to act because the statue was almost upon them. They pooled their minds as one and focused. Luminous ropes of energy soon sprouted from each of their hands. They created their own colours blue, red, green, orange and yellow. The ropes slithered towards the target and began to coil. The statue realised what was happening and sent a laser beams from its eyes to block the attack. But, the concentration from all five of them was too much. The twisting ropes honed in and wrapped around its ankles. The rainbow of coloured ropes choked like a Boa Constrictor. The giant tried as it might but couldn't break free. It was working.

The monster's stride became laboured and the constant restricting stranglehold pulled its limbs tighter together. The colossal metal beast seemed to screech, and soon had no stride, so tumbled over and crashed to the ground. The whole of the inside of the cave shook violently. When the dust began to clear, the statue struggled in the dirt. Two of the ropes uncoiled from the legs and slithered up to the creature's neck. The blue and green luminous snake wrapped around the throat. The beast tried its best to pull the tightening noose apart, and was beginning to gain. So more strands uncoiled from the ankles and joined in, adding to the strength of the noose. Sounds of choking erupted from deep in the throat of the stone monster as it defied death! But the noose tightened and tightened – the concentration of the youths' minds was at its highest. It writhed and wrestled for survival – the grey of the monster against the bright vibrant colours of the rope.

The creature took one last lunge, and that was it. The rope crushed its neck with a huge C-R-A-C-K, and what sounded like a scream deep within its soul. The head broke off and tumbled to the ground with a THUMP! The yellow eyes inside its head, faded. The rest of its body stopped struggling and the whole thing went silent.

The five teenagers fell back. They looked on as they sat up panting and drained. It just looked like a huge boulder now that had been there for thousands of years. It took them a little while to gain some composure.

'Look how harmless it looks now,' Sarah uttered, coughing up dust.

'It wasn't harmless a minute ago, that's for sure.' Keiron commented.

'Boy, that was hard,' Joseph admitted. 'Wouldn't want to be doing that too often.'

'You're not wrong there,' Jenna gushed, dusting down her armour.

'We pulled together that's the main thing,' Steve said looking chuffed.

'Jesus, what next?' Keiron gasped.

'Who knows? Knowing our luck, a nest of dragons,' Sarah added comically.

'Don't tempt fate,' Joseph said, still breathing hard. 'I'm expecting anything and everything from now on.'

Chapter 19

The Accelerator

Drained of strength and pondering on what was coming next, the five friends got to their feet.

'How's your head feeling now, Steve?' Keiron asked checking up on his friend's wellbeing.

'Probably as bad as yours,' he said with a heavy sigh, feeling the bandage that was now as black as the cave.

'Mine is thumping, so yours must be exploding,' Keiron said.

'Not too bad actually, all this chaos must have calmed me down,' Steve said with a shrug of the shoulders.

'God, is that it?' Sarah was edging forward and muttering to herself. The others now intrigued, followed her line of vision.

Just beyond the stricken statue, something else featured in the cavern. At first it was inconspicuous and underwhelming. It stood approximately thirty metres ahead, at the far corner of the cave. All five of them looked on in disappointment. If this was the machine they'd been searching for; it was nothing like they'd expected. Joseph looked on dismissively.

'That's the Accelerator?' Joseph said. 'That's what we've been risking life and limb for?' The disappointment was heavy in his tone. He stood vacantly, peering at the strange object. In fact it wasn't even a machine at all. It resembled more of a tree! The outer skin was a mixture of purple and brown. There were no switches or buttons that the team could make out. They moved in closer to get a better look. The five of them stood in a semi-circle.

The Accelerator itself was roughly two metres high. It had a trunk, which twisted from its thick root and out to strangely distorted arms. These resembled a multi-limbed monster that seemed to be reaching towards the group. On various parts of these branches were insets – the same size and shape of the discs. Keiron let out a full giggle.

'I was expecting some mad scientist's doomsday machine,' Keiron gasped. 'You know, all flashing lights and dials. But this…'

'Doesn't look like something that could change the world,' Sarah said sceptically. 'It feels like it wants to be hugged.' Steve looked at her with a quirky expression.

'You a hippie or something?' he said sarcastically.

'I agree with Sarah, it resembles a prop from a theatre,' Jenna exclaimed. 'I can't imagine this bringing down Earth's defences.' Joseph studied it and realised something that no one else had seen.

'Well, whatever it is, I don't know if you lot have noticed, but… it has six places to set the discs, and… there are only five of us,' he said dryly.

'Wha-what does that mean?' Sarah uttered, the nervousness clear in her voice. Keiron raised his eyebrows with suspicion.

'There can't be six of us, surely?' Steve interjected. 'Only five of us came down here, and only five of us were abducted in the first place.'

'I can't see any other explanation,' Joseph added with a shrug of his shoulders.

'Okay, who is the other one, then?' Jenna probed.

'Yeah, who?' Sarah echoed.

'Gotta be Zaan, hasn't it?' Keiron reasoned. 'He must have followed us down.'

'Why hasn't he showed himself, then?' Steve quizzed.

'No, there's got to be another explanation,' Jenna joined in.

'If he could've come down – he'd have done it on his own. He wouldn't even have needed us in the first place,' Sarah said sensibly. There were nods of agreement.

'Hold on, can you feel that?' Joseph cut in.

'Wha… what are you on about, Joe? Shut up, you're frightening me,' Jenna admitted. No one moved – the room fell silent for a few moments. All five of them were trembling, even though they would never admit it.

'There's someone else in here,' Sarah said shakily with eyes closed, her voice cutting through the silence.

'Someone… or something?' Jenna asked, easing back half a step. The cave, all of a sudden, felt more sinister. Their flashlights were trained on the strange tree object, but the shadows cast on the walls that surrounded them were evil.

'I-I can feel a presence,' Keiron stammered.

'Me too,' Joseph agreed.

'Who… who are you?' Steve called out to the darkness.

'Yeah, don't hide like a coward, step into our light so we can see you,' Keiron barked trying it build up courage, but not totally convincing anyone.

'Please, who are you?' Joseph said in a friendlier refrain. 'We don't mean to harm you. We are your friends,' Joseph continued.

'I wouldn't say that,' Sarah whispered. Nothing was said for a few moments.

'Please,' Jenna's voice surprised everyone, 'tell us who you are and what you're doing here?' The shaky shafts of light from their flashlights gave away their fear.

'I-am-Moss,' the voice eventually spoke up. It wasn't verbally audible. It was more like a collective assault inside each of the their minds. Each of the team found it hard to breathe.

'Oh this is too weird,' Steve responded, whipping his head in every direction to try and see whatever was sending the signal. 'Is that the tree talking?'

'I don't think so,' Keiron commented.

'I-I'm scared,' Jenna said, her trembling body obvious.

'Me too.' Sarah said as she gripped Jenna's arm; the two held each other for comfort.

'Okay, what… are you, Moss? Are you an animal or a vegetable?' Keiron chipped in. Steve looked at him incredulously, right eyebrow arched. There was a long silence again and then it spoke again.

'I-am-Moss,' the voice repeated, washing through their minds like a ribbon of water pushing down stream.

'It's Moss, then?' Steve smirked as Jenna dug him in the ribs.

'Moss, what do you want with us?' Keiron kept up the questions, but getting really annoyed. He'd been through enough and this was just too much to work out right now.

'I-need-you.' It spoke simply as if it knew who they were and what it was doing here.

'Need us... need us for what?' Steve said.

'Yeah, need us for what?' Sarah couldn't hold back.

'Hold on, guys we're bombarding it with too many questions,' Jenna said. 'Just one of us speak to it.'

'Let Joseph ask,' Steve said, surprising everyone.

Joseph composed himself. 'Are you from Ether World?' he blurted out.

Again, another pause. 'I-have-been-waiting-a-long-time,' it said, making absolutely no sense to them.

'This is getting us nowhere,' Steve said angrily. 'I don't...'

'Place-your-discs-in-the-Accelerator.' Moss's command stopped Steve in his tracks.

'Wha...?' Steve was confused.

'You are the Accelerator?' Keiron said. Now everything felt so real.

'No,' Jenna snapped. 'I'm not doing it. If we do, Earth will be invaded by Ether World and everyone will be killed,' Jenna admitted truthfully, 'If we don't, they will kill our families on Ether World. We can't commit to anything,' she said, crying and trembling at the same time.

'There-is-another-way,' the voice spoke. Now the silence was mirrored from the teenagers.

'Another way? Why should we trust you?' Joseph stepped up closer. 'You won't even tell us who you are. What other way?'

'I-am-Moss.'

'For God's sake, what does that mean?' Jenna screeched angrily. 'We know who you are, you bloody stupid thing.' Jenna voiced her anger.

Joseph was working things out in his mind, and realised the voice sounded kind of child-like. Were they dealing with an alien who was a child? He'd heard something similar on a Star Trek episode, but dismissed it as foolish.

'I-can-change-everything.' Joseph listened to it again and it did sound infantile.

'This is crazy!' Keiron was ready with an outburst.

Joseph raised up his hand to stop him. He mouthed to him to hold on and tapped a finger to his temple. He glanced at the others and gave them the same mimic. They had no idea what he was planning.

'Moss, how can you change everything?' Joseph talked softly. 'What would you do?'

'I-can-make-things-better-in-Ether-World-and-stop-Earth -from-being-attacked-by-this-other-enemy.'

Joseph looked seriously at the others. Whatever this situation was, it wasn't to be joked about.

'That's what we want, Moss.' Joseph was leading it through his plan to extract the information. 'How do we do that? Tell us?'

'As-I-said, place-your-discs-into-the-Accelerator – that-is-all-you-need-to-do.'

'Let me speak with my friends privately, Moss, and we'll give you our answer. But, you must not listen in on our conversation,' Joseph insisted, 'this is a private conversation.'

'Moss-will-not-listen-to-your-conversation.'

The five kids made their way over to the far corner of the cave. They huddled into a circle, as tight together as was possible.

'What do you think, guys?' Joseph asked with a stern look. 'Can we trust it, do you think?'

'What do you think it's going to do, exactly?' Keiron hissed urgently, his eyes widening in the white light.

'We've got no guarantees,' Steve added, 'but when we start this thing – there'll be no going back.'

'Jenna?' Joseph looked at her tired eyes. 'What do you think?'

'I don't know, what choice do we have?' she replied. 'It's scary either way.'

'Sarah?' Joseph flicked his gaze to her.

'God... I'm scared either way too,' she said, her bottom lip trembling. 'I'll go with the rest of you guys.'

'I'm with Sarah. Whatever you guys decide, I'll go with the flow,' Jenna said.

'What about you?' Steve pointed his question to Joseph.

'I really don't think we have much of a choice. I think we have to trust this Moss thingy,' Joseph admitted. 'Whichever way we go, is a bad direction. Ether World invading! This other threat from another world, that's invading us too. There's also our families, up there in danger from Zaan and the elders on Ether World. Or the families we have right here on Earth, in danger too, if they're still alive. We can't do nothing at all, and if we do something it could all go horribly wrong. The only hope we have is, Moss, as far as I can see,' he said. 'There's something about Moss that I believe in, don't ask me why.'

'We have to chance it then,' Keiron agreed, the decision made as far as he was concerned.

'I think you're right,' Jenna also agreed.

'I don't know,' Steve said honestly.

'I'm scared either way,' Jenna sobbed.

'Do we go with a vote?' There was nodding from everyone.

'Hands up who's willing to do what Moss is asking…?'

But before anyone could react, there was an explosion that shook the cave and reverberated the mineshaft. Everyone steadied themselves, and managed to stand upright. There was a huge cloud of dust and the sound of cracking timber and falling rocks.

'Oh my God,' Sarah screamed.

'They're here,' Keiron gasped.

'No time to lose – hands up,' Joseph shouted, coughing and spluttering. Everyone raised an arm. 'Moss, what do we do?' he shouted through the clouds of dust.

'Place-your-disks-on-the-Accelerator,' it said calmly.

'Come on, do as it says, guys!' Joseph screeched with a dry throat and mouth. There was such a heavy dust cloud that no one could see the tree. Joseph clambered towards it as another blast exploded the mine.

'COME ON,' Steve shouted. Each one of them – Keiron, Jenna, Sarah, Steve and Joseph – traced their way to the tree.

'We all here?' Keiron bellowed. 'Shout out your names.'

'Jenna.'

'Steve.'

'Joseph.'

'Sarah.'

'Me,' Keiron added.

The grey dust that engulfed the cavern began to subside, and the tree was once again visible. Without wasting any more time, the five friends each stepped forward and placed their disks on the branches. Once the last one was placed, they stepped back. There was the sound of activity deep inside the mine and they knew it wouldn't be long before they'd be captured.

'Moss, there's one space left. Who's that for?' Steve shouted dryly.

'That will be mine.' A voice came from behind them and when they turned to face whoever it was... they were flabbergasted.

'Mr Brown,' they all said simultaneously. Joseph couldn't believe it – it was his history teacher. He was also Keiron's next-door neighbour and Jenna's music teacher. It appeared that Mr Brown was also Sarah's dance teacher and, Steve's football coach.

He simply walked forward and said, 'All will be explained.' He then put his disc on the final branch and everything faded into blackness.

Chapter 20

The Mind Doctor

'Joseph! Joseph, can you hear me? It's all over, you can open your eyes.' Joseph slowly opened his lids a crack, the light was blinding. He felt himself hiss with the sudden pain to his eyeballs.

'Wha... what's happening?' he croaked. He looked around the room and didn't recognise anything. Also, he was lying on a recliner chair, in what appeared to be a doctor's study, but different somehow to any doctor he'd ever visited. Joseph was about to move, but found he was restricted – his body was strapped in but his arms were free.

'What's going on?' he said as he reached up and felt that his head was in some kind of headrest. There weren't any wires connected to him only pulsing lights to each side. He lifted himself into a sitting position, and felt off balance.

'Steady, Joseph, don't sit up so quickly,' said a man in a soothing tone. Joseph peered across at the person talking to him, and was shocked!

'Mr Brown?' he said. 'Where am I and what am I doing here?' Joseph was confused and worried.

'Hi, Joseph, do you remember anything about what happened to you recently?' Mr Brown was sitting on a chair, next to his.

'I was in your history class and you were asking me questions,' Joseph remembered. 'What am I doing here, Mr Brown?' Joseph was confused. 'This is not your classroom.'

'Hold on, let me free you up from the straps and I'll explain everything,' he said and tore away the velcro. 'I am Mr Brown, but I'm not your history teacher.' Joseph looked even more confused. 'I am a psychiatrist,' he spoke calmly. Joseph felt his stomach tighten. 'You've been bullied for quite some time and your parents were worried and came to me for help.'

'My parents – my parents are okay, then?' Joseph interrupted, remembering the explosions. His memories were slowly coming back.

'Yes. Yes, Joseph, your parents are fine. I've put you onto a programme that's a new concept,' Mr Brown continued. 'I call it the DISC programme. It's meant to build up your confidence, self-esteem and give you a better quality of life. Everything you've experienced in the past few hours, were through my programme.'

'So, the disc didn't send me to Ether World?' Joseph questioned, feeling silly now.

'I'm afraid not, no,' Mr Brown sympathised.

'So Zaan isn't real either?' Joseph asked. 'So the elders and the sabre-tooth all…?'

'No, Zaan is just another part of this programme, and so was everything else.'

'What about the other people in there: Jenna, Steve, Keiron and Sarah?' Joseph was feeling a let down. 'I suppose they were all in the programme too?' He hated the thought of that. He got on well with them and now they were only a programmed chip.

'No, actually they are real. In fact, they are in the same programme as you, because they were getting bullied too,' Mr Brown told him.

'Well, what happens now then? Did it work?' Joseph enquired. 'Am I cured?'

'I rather think it did. Do you feel more confident now? From what I monitored on screen, you seemed to really get into the events of the story,' Mr Brown said excitedly, 'I've been developing this programme for many years and now it's finally working.' He was almost jumping out of his chair.

'I do, I feel different now. But all the skills I learned in there won't happen for real though. The flying and powers I had?' Joseph looked at him sceptically.

'Not the flying and super powers part,' he smiled, 'but the self-defence software is a new concept that you will have learned.' Mr Brown added, 'like I said, it's a new programme that only you five have experienced so far. I'm excited see how you will improve over the next few weeks.'

'How did I get here in the first place… Oh, I remember, I was supposed to drop in for a check up with a specialist,' he remembered.

'Yes, if you can recall, a nurse gave you a tablet to swallow – with the express permission from your parents, of course,' Mr Brown added.

'That's right, and then everything went weird from there,' Joseph recalled. 'But it all felt so real.'

'It was supposed to. The whole experience was put together to make the occupier of the programme feel that he or she was totally submerged in the adventure. There was a short surge of power at one point, but it didn't effect or interfere with the running of the protocols.'

'Will I have to come back?' Joseph enquired.

'You'll have to pop back for a couple of appointments for me to keep an eye on you,' Mr Brown assured him. 'But I don't foresee any problems,' he said.

'Can I see my parents now?' Joseph really needed to make sure they were all right.

'Of course you can. Are you all right to stand up?' he asked.

'I think so,' Joseph said settling his feet on the floor. 'Yeah, I'm okay.'

'Your parents are outside waiting for you. Off you go then and I'll see you next week, the receptionist will give you an appointment card. Bye now,' Mr Brown said as he opened the door for him.

He was right. Joseph's mum and dad were waiting. He stepped out of Mr Brown's office, and saw his parents sitting there looking really anxious. He walked up to them and his mother gave him the biggest hug he'd ever experienced.

'Take it easy, Mum, I need to breathe you know,' he said, his head buried in her shoulder. He broke away and his dad rubbed his back in a gesture of support. But Joseph turned and hugged him too.

'That was a mad experience,' Joseph said.

'Are you all right, love?' his mother asked, still concerned. 'You're not …you know, traumatised?' Joseph let out a big laugh and hugged her again.

'I'm fine, Mum, honestly,' he said, peering into her glassy eyes. Suddenly Mr Brown appeared and called his parents in, but asked him to stay outside for a moment. Joseph sat quietly and suddenly felt a pair of eyes looking at him. When he turned to find out who was staring, he saw Jenna. Joseph was astonished.

'Jenna,' he called in more of a whisper.

'Hi, Joseph. Crazy, huh?' she said, smiling. 'The others are here too.'

'They are? Mr Brown said you were all here. I suppose I should call him Doctor Brown,' he added. When Joseph looked further up the corridor he could plainly see Keiron, Steve and Sarah. He gave them a wave, and they each returned the compliment. A moment or two later, Dr Brown appeared again, and with him the parents of each of them. Everyone made their way to the car park, and soon they all went their own way. Joseph sat in the back of the car thinking about what had taken place. It was still hard for him to conceive the DISC programme and the experiment he'd been involved in. The evening was spent being pampered by his parents, with sweets and chocolates. They even let him watch his favourite television series.

Joseph woke up the next morning feeling really different. The first thing he did was to touch his chest. It was crazy, but he thought he could still feel the outline of the disc there. It was so real to his touch. He climbed out of bed and made his way downstairs, to the biggest breakfast he'd ever had. It took him a while to get away from his mother, and go to school. The strangest thing was, in school, the teacher who took history was Mrs Jenkins, and Joseph felt kind of sad. The day flew by and when the bell went, Joseph left school without feeling nervous at all. He knew he would have to walk through the woods again, and he knew who would be there. It was sunny outside, which had cleared up from rain that morning. The other kids left on the bus and Joseph walked through the treeline as usual. He came across the familiar patch of ground, but it didn't send a shiver through him, or make him feel sick today.

And there they were – the Mackenzie brothers. His stomach churned, just for a moment and then the nervousness melted away. Joseph felt confident and in control, just like Dr Brown had said. He took a deep breath.

'Well, look who's come back to school? Hope you haven't been ill,' Jedd chuckled. Joseph went to side step them, but was blocked.

'Where do you think you're going, mate?' Gary said and poked Joseph in the chest. 'There's a nice patch of mud waiting for you, right there,' Jedd said, as Gary burst into a full belly laugh. 'It's especially wet for a nice dip,' Jedd explained.

'Let me get by – I'm warning you two,' Joseph said, the confidence oozing through his veins. Did the experiment work, Joseph thought. A tiny seed of doubt pulled at him, but was dismissed.

'What?' Gary was almost lost for words.

'You're warning us?' Jedd retorted and reached out with his right hand to grab him. Joseph countered the attack by gripping his right wrist and twisting it over. Jedd couldn't do anything about it and had to follow the motion of his arm by bending over double. A swift sidekick propelled Jedd at such speed that he flipped over and fell straight into the mud. It all happened so quickly that Gary didn't have time to process it. He was then filled with anger and lunged at Joseph. Joseph ducked and stepped to one side. Gary, having missed turned and charged at him again. He surged forward like a steam train, while Joseph waited for the right moment. At the last second, he simply jumped out of the way. Gary went sprawling into the mud puddle and landed on top of his brother. Who was knocked back and tumbled into the wet sticky soil again.

Eventually they got to their feet and waded out, covered in brown, smelly mud. Joseph took a fighter's stance ready for the next bout. But the brothers were apprehensive and didn't know how to handle this new Joseph.

'Do you want some more?' he said with a huge grin on his face and jerked forward in a mock attack. The two brothers flinched and fell back in the puddle. This day was the best day of his life. He actually had the two Mackenzie brothers scared of him! They never bothered him again after that, and they didn't pick on anyone else either – just in case Joseph got to know about it.

The weeks went on and one Saturday while Joseph was walking to town, he felt and heard something.

'Joseph, Jenna's in trouble, we need your help.' Joseph could hear Sarah's voice as plain as day, and he could still feel the disc, the feeling hadn't gone away.

'Sarah, is that you? How can I hear you?' he said, feeling really confused.

'I don't know, it's the same with me. I can hear you, Steve and Keiron,' she said with a tremble in her voice.

'This isn't supposed to happen,' he said, trying to make sense of it all, 'but I'll come right away.' Joseph could suddenly feel the hard shell wrap around his body. He looked in the nearest shop window. He could plainly see the familiar white armoured suit he wore in the sessions with Dr Brown. This was ridiculous; surely he would stand out, exposed like this. But the shoppers that walked past him didn't seem to notice, so he presumed they could only see his normal clothes.

What was going on? Was the disc somehow actually inside him for real? The questions were mounting up. He had to find Sarah first of all. Where did he have to go? Suddenly his visor appeared and the co-ordinates flashed up. It was time to go.

This was definitely real!